Charles Dickens

Beautiful Stories about Children

ISBN/EAN: 9783337417802

Printed in Europe, USA, Canada, Australia, Japan

Cover: Foto ©Andreas Hilbeck / pixelio.de

More available books at **www.hansebooks.com**

Charles Dickens

Beautiful Stories about Children

BEAUTIFUL STORIES

...ABOUT...

CHILDREN

BY CHARLES DICKENS

RETOLD BY

HIS GRANDDAUGHTER AND OTHERS

SUPERBLY ILLUSTRATED

WITH NEARLY 100

NEW COLOR PLATES, HALF-TONES AND PEN SKETCHES

MADE ESPECIALLY BY FAMOUS ARTISTS

FOR THESE STORIES

THIS BOOK CONTAINS THE MOST CHARMING PORTRAYALS
OF CHILD-CHARACTER FROM THE IMMORTAL
WORKS OF THE GREAT AUTHOR

THE JOHN C. WINSTON CO.,

CHICAGO, PHILADELPHIA, TORONTO.

CHARLES DICKENS.

"It was Dickens who made it popular to keep Christmas with acts of helpfulness to the poor. Every barefooted boy and girl in the streets of England and America to-day fares a little better, gets fewer cuffs and more pudding because Charles Dickens wrote. He has softened the hearts of more than a generation. He made charity fashionable and awakened the pity and brotherly love of millions of people."

CONTENTS.

List of Original Illustrations.

XIII

LIST OF LITHOGRAPH PLATES

AND FULL-PAGE HALF-TONE ILLUSTRATIONS.

Little Nell.

THE house was one of those receptacles for old and curious things, which seem to crouch in odd corners of the town, and to hide their musty treasures from the public eye in jealousy and distrust. There were suits of mail standing like ghosts in armor, here and there; fantastic carvings brought from monkish cloisters; rusty weapons of various kinds; distorted figures in china, and wood, and iron and ivory; tapestry, and strange furniture that might have been designed in dreams; and in the old, dark, murky rooms there lived alone together an old man and a child—his grandchild, Little Nell. Solitary and monotonous as was her life, the innocent and cheerful spirit of the child found happiness in all things, and through the dim rooms of the old curiosity shop

LITTLE NELL.

Little Nell went singing, moving with gay and lightsome step.

But gradually over the old man, to whom she was so tenderly attached, there stole a sad change. He became thoughtful, dejected, and wretched. He had no sleep or rest but that which he took by day in his easy chair; for every night, and all night long, he was away from home. To the child it seemed that her grandfather's love for her increased, even with the hidden grief by which she saw him struck down. And to see him sorrowful, and not to know the cause of his sorrow; to see him growing pale and weak under his agony of mind, so weighed upon her gentle spirit that at times she felt as though her heart must break.

At last the time came when the old man's feeble frame could bear up no longer against his hidden care. A raging fever seized him, and, as he lay delirious or insensible through many weeks, Nell learned that the house which sheltered them was theirs no longer; that in the future they would be very poor; that they would scarcely have bread to eat.

At length the old man began to mend, but his mind was weakened.

He would sit for hours together, with Nell's small hand in his, playing with the fingers, and sometimes stopping to smooth her hair or kiss her brow; and when he saw that tears were glistening in her eyes he would look amazed. As the time drew near when they must leave the house, he made no reference to the necessity of finding other shelter. An indistinct idea he had that the child was desolate and in need of help; though he seemed unable to contemplate their real position more distinctly. But a change came upon him one evening as he and Nell sat silently together.

"Let us speak softly, Nell," he said. "Hush! for if they knew our purpose they would say that I was mad, and take thee from me. We will not stop here another day. We will travel afoot through the fields and woods, and trust ourselves to God in the places where He dwells. To-mor-

DEAR GENTLE, PATIENT, NOBLE NELL

Old Curiosity Shop

row morning, dear, we'll turn our faces from this scene of sorrow, and be as free and happy as the birds."

The child's heart beat high with hope and confidence. She had no thought of hunger, or cold, or thirst, or suffering. To her it seemed that they might beg their way from door to door in happiness, so that they were together.

When the day began to glimmer they stole out of the house, and, passing into the street, stood still.

"Which way?" asked the child.

The old man looked irresolutely and helplessly at her, and shook his head. It was plain that she was thenceforth his guide and leader. The child felt it, but had no doubts or misgivings, and, putting her hand in his, led him gently away. Forth from the city, while it yet slumbered, went the two poor adventurers, wandering they knew not whither.

They passed through the long, deserted streets, in the glad light of early morning, until these streets dwindled away, and the open country was about them. They walked all day, and slept that night at a small cottage where beds were let to travelers. The sun was setting on the second day of their journey, and they were jaded and worn out with walking, when, following a path which led through a churchyard to the town where they were to spend the night, they fell in with two traveling showmen, exhibitors of a Punch and Judy show. They raised their eyes when the old man and his young companion were close upon them. One of them, the actual exhibitor, no doubt, was a little, merry-faced man with a twinkling eye and a red nose, who seemed to have unconsciously imbibed something of his hero's character. The other—that was he who took the money—had rather a careful and cautious look, which was perhaps inseparable from his occupation also.

THE DEPARTURE OF LITTLE NELL AND HER GRANDFATHER.

The merry man was the first to greet the strangers with a nod; and following the old man's eyes, he observed that perhaps that was the first time he had seen a Punch off the stage. (Punch, it may be remarked, seemed to be pointing with the tip of his cap to a most flourishing epitaph, and to be chuckling over it with all his heart.)

"Why do you come here to do this?" said the old man, sitting down beside them, and looking at the figures with extreme delight.

"Why, you see," rejoined the little man, "we're putting up for to-night at the public house yonder, and it wouldn't do to let 'em see the present company undergoing repair."

"No!" cried the old man, making signs to Nell to listen, "why not, eh? why not?"

"Because it would destroy all the delusion and take away all the interest, wouldn't it?" replied the man. "Would you care a ha'penny for the Lord Chancellor if you know'd him in private and without his wig?—certainly not."

"Good!" said the old man, venturing to touch one of the puppets, and drawing away his hand with a shrill laugh. "Are you going to show 'em to-night—are you?"

"That is the intention, governor," replied the other "and unless I'm much mistaken, Tommy Codlin is a-calculating at this minute what we've lost through your coming upon us. Cheer up, Tommy, it can't be much."

The little man accompanied these latter words with a wink, expressive of the estimate he had formed of the travelers' pocketbook.

To this Mr. Codlin, who had a surly, grumbling manner, replied, as he twitched Punch off the tombstone and flung him into the box:

"I don't care if we haven't lost a farden, but you're too

free. If you stood in front of the curtain and see the public's faces as I do, you'd know human natur' better.''

Turning over the figures in the box like one who knew and despised them, Mr. Codlin drew one forth and held it up for the inspection of his friend:

''Look here; here's all this Judy's clothes falling to pieces again. You haven't got a needle and thread, I suppose?''

THE EXHIBITORS OF THE PUNCH AND JUDY SHOW.

The little man shook his head and scratched it ruefully, as he contemplated this severe indisposition of a principal performer. Seeing that they were at a loss, the child said, timidly:

''I have a needle, sir, in my basket, and thread, too. Will you let me try to mend it for you? I think I could do it neater than you could.''

Even Mr. Codlin had nothing to urge against a proposal so seasonable. Nell, kneeling down beside the box, was soon busily engaged in her task, and accomplishing it to a miracle.

While she was thus engaged the merry little man looked at her with an interest which did not appear to be diminished when he glanced at her helpless companion. When she had finished her work he thanked her, and inquired whither they were traveling.

"N—no farther to-night, I think," said the child, looking toward her grandfather.

"If you're wanting a place to stop at," the man remarked, "I should advise you to take up at the same house with us. That's it. The long, low, white house there. It's very cheap."

When they had been refreshed the whole house hurried away into an empty stable where the show stood, and where, by the light of a few flaring candles stuck around a hoop which hung by a line from the ceiling, it was to be forthwith exhibited.

And now Mr. Thomas Codlin, after blowing away at the Pan's pipes, took his station on one side of the checked drapery which concealed the mover of the figures, and, putting his hands in his pockets, prepared to reply to all questions and remarks of Punch, and to make a dismal feint of being his most intimate private friend, of believing in him to the fullest and most unlimited extent, of knowing that he enjoyed day and night a merry and glorious existence in that temple, and that he was at all times and under every circumstance the same intelligent and joyful person that the spectators then beheld him.

The whole performance was applauded to the echo, and voluntary contributions were showered in with a liberality which testified yet more strongly to the general delight.

Among the laughter none was more loud and frequent than the old man's. Nell's was unheard, for she, poor child, with her head drooping on his shoulder, had fallen asleep, and slept too soundly to be roused by any of his efforts to awaken her to a participation in his glee.

The supper was very good, but she was too tired to eat, and yet would not leave the old man until she had kissed him in his bed. He, happily insensible to every care and anxiety, sat listening with a vacant smile and admiring face to all that his new friends said; and it was not until they retired, yawning, to their room that he followed the child upstairs.

She had little money, but it was very little, and when that was gone they must begin to beg. There was one piece of gold among it, and an emergency might come when its worth to them would be increased a hundredfold. It would be best to hide this coin, and never produce it unless their case was absolutely desperate, and no other resource was left them.

Her resolution taken, she sewed the piece of gold into her dress, and going to bed with a lighter heart sunk into a deep slumber.

"And where are you going to-day?" said the little man the following morning, addressing himself to Nell.

"Indeed I hardly know—we have not determined yet," replied the child.

"We're going on to the races," said the little man. "If that's your way and you like to have us for company, let us travel together. If you prefer going alone, only say the word and you'll find that we shan't trouble you.'

"We'll go with you," said the old man. "Nell—with them, with them."

The child considered for a moment, and reflecting that she must shortly beg, and could scarcely hope to do so at a better place than where crowds of rich ladies and gentlemen were assembled together for purposes of enjoyment and festivity, determined to accompany these men so far. She therefore thanked the little man for his offer, and said, glancing timidly toward his friend, that they would if there was no objection to their accompanying them as far as the race-town.

And with these men they traveled forward on the following day.

They made two long days' journey with their new companions, passing through villages and towns, and meeting upon one occasion with two young people walking upon stilts, who were also going to the races.

And now they had come to the time when they must beg their bread. Soon after sunrise the second morning she stole out, and, rambling into some fields at a short distance, plucked a few wild roses and such humble flowers, purposing to make them into little nosegays and offer them to the ladies in the carriages when the company arrived. Her thoughts were not idle while she was thus employed; when she returned and was seated beside the old man, tying her flowers together, while the two men lay dozing in a corner, she plucked him by the sleeve, and, slightly glancing toward them, said in a low voice:

"Grandfather, don't look at those I talk of, and don't seem as if I spoke of anything but what I am about. What was that you told me before we left the old house? That if they knew what we were going to do, they would say that you were mad, and part us?"

The old man turned to her with an aspect of wild terror; but she checked him by a look, and bidding him hold some flowers while she tied them up, and so bringing her lips closer to his ear, said:

"I know that was what you told me. You needn't speak, dear. I recollect it very well. It is not likely that I should forget it. Grandfather, these men I have heard suspect that we have secretly left our friends, and mean to carry us before some gentleman and have us taken care of and sent back. If you let your hand tremble so, we can never get away from them, but if you're only quiet now, we shall do so easily."

"How?" muttered the old man. "Dear Nell, how? They will shut me up in a stone-room, dark and cold, and chain me up to the wall, Nell—flog me with whips, and never let me see thee more!"

"You're trembling again," said the child. "Keep close to me all day. Never mind them, don't look at them, but me. I shall find a time when we can steal away. When I do, mind you come with me, and do not stop or speak a word. Hush! That's all."

"Halloo! what are you up to, my dear?" said Mr. Cod-lin, raising his head and yawning.

"Making some nosegays," the child replied; "I am going to try and sell some these three days of the races. Will you have one—as a present, I mean?"

Mr. Codlin would have risen to receive it, but the child hurried toward him and placed it in his hand, and he stuck it in his button-hole.

As the morning wore on, the tents at the race-course assumed a gayer and more brilliant appearance, and long lines of carriages came rolling softly on the turf. Black-eyed gypsy girls, hooded in showy handkerchiefs, sallied

forth to tell fortunes, and pale, slender women with con-
sumptive faces lingered upon the footsteps of ventriloquists
and conjurers, and counted the sixpences with anxious eyes
long before they were gained. As many of the children as
could be kept within bounds were stowed away, with all the
other signs of dirt and poverty, among the donkeys, carts,
and horses; and as many as could not be thus disposed of
ran in and out in all intricate spots, crept between people's
legs and carriage wheels, and came forth unharmed from
under horses' hoofs. The dancing-dogs, the stilts, the little
lady and the tall man, and all the other attractions, with
organs out of number and bands innumerable, emerged from
the holes and corners in which they had passed the night.
and flourished boldly in the sun.

Along the uncleared course Short led his party, sounding
the brazen trumpet and reveling in the voice of Punch; and
at his heels went Thomas Codlin, bearing the show as usual,
and keeping his eye on Nell and her grandfather, as they
rather lingered in the rear. The child bore upon her arm
the little basket with her flowers, and sometimes stopped,
with timid and modest looks, to offer them at some gay carriage; but alas! there were many bolder beggars there,
gypsies who promised husbands, and other adepts in their
trade; and although some ladies smiled gently as they shook
their heads, and others cried to the gentlemen beside them,
"See what a pretty face!" they let the pretty face pass on,
and never thought that it looked tired or hungry.

There was but one lady who seemed to understand
the child, and she was one who sat alone in a handsome
carriage, while two young men in dashing clothes, who had
just dismounted from it, talked and laughed loudly at a little distance, appearing to forget her, quite. There were many

ladies all around, but they turned their backs, or looked another away, or at the two young men (not unfavorably at *them*), and left her to herself. She motioned away a gypsy woman urgent to tell her fortune, saying that it was told already and had been for some years, but called the child toward her, and, taking her flowers, put money into her trembling hand, and bade her go home and keep at home.

Many a time they went up and down those long, long lines, seeing everything but the horses and the race; when

THEY LAID DOWN AT NIGHT WITH NOTHING BETWEEN THEM AND THE SKY.

the bell rung to clear the course, going back to rest among the carts and donkeys, and not coming out again until the heat was over. Many a time, too, was Punch displayed in the full zenith of his humor; but all this while the eye of Thomas Codlin was upon them, and to escape without notice was impracticable.

At length, late in the day, Mr. Codlin pitched the show in a convenient spot, and the spectators were soon in the very triumph of the scene.

If they were ever to get away unseen, that was the very moment. Short was plying the quarter-staves vigorously

and knocking the characters in the fury of the combat against
the sides of the show, the people were looking on with laughing faces, and Mr. Codlin had relaxed into a grim smile as
his roving eye detected hands going into waistcoat pockets.
If they were ever to get away unseen, that was the very moment. They seized it, and fled.

They made a path through booths and carriages and
throngs of people, and never once stopped to look behind.
The bell was ringing, and the course was cleared by the time
they reached the ropes, but they dashed across it, insensible
to the shouts and screeching that assailed them for breaking
in upon its sanctity, and, creeping under the brow of the hill
at a quick pace, made for the open fields.

That night they reached a little village in a woody hollow. The village schoolmaster, a good and gentle man,
pitying their weariness, and attracted by the child's sweet-
ness and modesty, gave them a lodging for the night; nor
would he let them leave him until two days more had passed.

They journeyed on, when the time came that they must
wander forth again, by pleasant country lanes; and as they
passed, watching the birds that perched and twittered in the
branches overhead, or listening to the songs that broke the
happy silence, their hearts were tranquil and serene. But
by-and-by they came to a long winding road which length-
ened out far into the distance, and though they still kept on,
it was at a much slower pace, for they were now very weary
and fatigued.

The afternoon had worn away into a beautiful evening,
when they arrived at a point where the road made a sharp
turn and struck across a common. On the border of this
common, and close to the hedge which divided it from the
cultivated fields, a caravan was drawn up to rest; upon

which, by reason of its situation, they came so suddenly
that they could not have avoided it if they would.

It was not a shabby, dingy, dusty cart, but a smart
little house upon wheels, with white dimity curtains festoon-
ing the windows, and window-shutters of green picked out
with panels
of a staring
red, in which
happily-con-
trasted
colors the
whole con-
cern shone
brilliant.
Neither was
it a poor
caravan
drawn by a
single
donkey or
emaciated
horse, for a

"UPON ONE OCCASION, THEY MET TWO YOUNG PEOPLE
WALKING ON STILTS."

pair of horses in pretty good condition were released
from the shafts and grazing on the frouzy grass. Neither
was it a gypsy caravan, for at the open door (graced with
a bright brass knocker) sat a Christian lady, stout and
comfortable to look upon, who wore a large bonnet trembling with bows. And that it was not an unprovided or
destitute caravan was clear from this lady's occupation,
which was the very pleasant and refreshing one of taking tea.
The tea-things, including a bottle of rather suspicious
character and a cold knuckle of ham, were set forth upon a

drum, covered with a white napkin; and there, as if at the most convenient round-table in all the world, sat this roving lady, taking her tea and enjoying the prospect.

It happened at that moment that the lady of the caravan had her cup (which, that everything about her might be of a stout and comfortable kind, was a breakfast cup) to her

MRS. JARLEY.

lips, and that having her eyes lifted to the sky in her enjoyment of the full flavor of her tea, it happened that being thus agreeably en-gaged, she did not see the travelers when they first came up. It was not until she was in the act of setting down the cup, and drawing a long breath after the ex-ertion of causing its con-tents to disappear, that the lady of the caravan beheld an old man and a young child walking slowly by, and glancing at her proceedings with eyes of modest but hungry admiration.

"Hey?" cried the lady of the caravan, scooping the crumbs out of her lap and swallowing the same before wiping her lips. "Yes, to be sure—who won the Helter-Skelter Plate, child?" "Won what, ma'am?" asked Nell.

"The Helter-Skelter Plate at the races, child—the plate that was run for on the second day."

"On the second day, ma'am?"

"Second day! Yes, second day," repeated the lady, with an air of impatience. "Can't you say who won the Helter-Skelter Plate when you're asked the question civilly?"

"I don't know, ma'am."

"Don't know!" repeated the lady of the caravan; "why, you were there. I saw you with my own eyes."

Nell was not a little alarmed to hear this, supposing that the lady might be intimately acquainted with the firm of Short and Codlin; but what followed tended to reassure her.

"And very sorry I was," said the lady of the caravan, "to see you in company with a Punch—a low, practical, vulgar wretch, that people should scorn to look at."

"I was not there by choice," returned the child; "we didn't know our way, and the two men were very kind to us, and let us travel with them. Do you—do you know them, ma'am?"

"Know 'em child?" cried the lady of the caravan, in a sort of shriek. "Know *them!* But you're young and inexperienced, and that's your excuse for asking sich a question. Do I look as if I know'd 'em? Does the caravan look as if *it* know'd 'em?"

"No, ma'am, no," said the child, fearing she had committed some grievous fault. "I beg your pardon."

The lady of the caravan was in the act of gathering her

tea equipage together preparatory to clearing the table, but noting the child's anxious manner, she hesitated and stopped. The child courtesied, and giving her hand to the old man, had already got some fifty yards or so away, when the lady of the caravan called to her to return.

"Come nearer, nearer still," said she, beckoning to her to ascend the steps. "Are you hungry, child?"

"Not very, but we are tired, and it's—it *is* a long way—"

"Well, hungry or not, you had better have some tea," rejoined her new acquaintance. "I suppose you are agreeable to that, old gentleman?"

The grandfather humbly pulled off his hat and thanked her. The lady of the caravan then bade him come up the steps likewise, but the drum proving an inconvenient table for two, they descended again, and sat upon the grass, where she handed down to them the tea-tray, the bread and butter, and the knuckle of ham.

"Set 'em out near the hind wheels, child, that's the best place," said their friend, superintending the arrangements from above. "Now hand up the tea-pot for a little more hot water and a pinch of fresh tea, and then both of you eat and drink as much as you can, and don't spare anything; that's all I ask of you."

The mistress of the caravan, saying the girl and her grandfather could not be very heavy, invited them to go along with them for a while, for which Nell thanked her with unaffected earnestness.

When they had traveled slowly forward for some short distance, Nell ventured to steal a look round the caravan and observe it more closely. One half of it—that moiety in which the comfortable proprietress was then seated—was

3

carpeted, and so partitioned off at the farther end as to ac-
commodate a sleeping-place, constructed after the fashion of
a berth on board ship, which was shaded, like the little windows, with fair white curtains, and looked comfortable
enough, though by what kind of gymnastic exercise the
lady of the caravan ever contrived to get into it was an un-
fathomable mystery. The other half served for a kitchen, and
was fitted up with a stove whose small chimney passed
through the roof.

The mistress sat looking at the child for a long time in
silence, and then, getting up, brought out from a corner a
large roll of canvas about a yard in width, which she laid
upon the floor and spread open with her foot until it nearly
reached from one end of the caravan to the other.

"There, child," she said, "read that."

Nell walked down it, and read aloud, in enormous black
letters, the inscription, "JARLEY'S WAX-WORK."

"Read it again," said the lady, complacently.

"Jarley's Wax-work," repeated Nell.

"That's me," said the lady. "I am Mrs. Jarley."

Giving the child an encouraging look, the lady of the
caravan unfolded another scroll, whereon was the inscription ; "One hundred figures the full size of life;" and then
another scroll, on which was written, "The only stupendous
collection of real wax-work in the world;" and then several
smaller scrolls, with such inscriptions as "Now exhibiting
within"—"The genuine and only Jarley"—"Jarley's unrivaled collection"—"Jarley is the delight of the Nobility
and Gentry"—"The Royal Family are the patrons of
Jarley." When she had exhibited these leviathans of public
announcement to the astonished child she brought forth
specimens of the lesser fry in the shape of handbills, some

of which were couched in the form of parodies on popular melodies, as "Believe me if all Jarley's wax-work so rare" —"I saw thy show in youthful prime"—"Over the water to Jarley;" while, to consult all tastes, others were composed with a view to the lighter and more facetious spirits, as a parody on the favorite air of "If I had a donkey," beginning

> If I know'd a donkey wot wouldn't go
> To see MRS. JARLEY'S wax work show,
> Do you think I'd acknowledge him?
> Oh no, no!
>   Then run to Jarley's——

besides several compositions in prose, purporting to be dialogues between the Emperor of China and an oyster.

"I never saw any wax-work, ma'am," said Nell. "Is it funnier than Punch?"

"Funnier!" said Mrs. Jarley, in a shrill voice. "It is not funny at all."

"Oh!" said Nell, with all possible humility.

"It isn't funny at all," repeated Mrs. Jarley. "It's calm and—what's that word again—critical?—no—classical, that's it —it's calm and classical. No low beatings and knockings about, no jokings and squeakings like your precious Punches,

WITH A WILLOW WAND NELL POINTED OUT THE CHARACTERS IN MRS. JARLEY'S WAX-WORK.

but always the same, with a constantly unchanging air of

coldness and gentility; and so like life that, if wax-work only spoke and walked about, you'd hardly know the difference. I won't go so far as to say that, as it is, I've seen wax-work quite like life, but I've certainly seen some life that was exactly like wax-work."

This conference at length concluded, she beckoned Nell to sit down.

"And the old gentleman, too," said Mrs. Jarley; "for I want to have a word with him. Do you want a good situation for your grand-daughter, master? If you do, I can put her in the way of getting one. What do you say?"

"I can't leave her," answered the old man. "We can't separate. What would become of me without her?"

"If you're really disposed to employ yourself," said Mrs. Jarley, "there would be plenty for you to do in the way of helping to dust the figures, and take the checks, and so forth. What I want your grand-daughter for is to point 'em out to the company; they would be soon learned, and she has a way with her that people wouldn't think unpleasant, though she *does* come after me; for I've been always accustomed to go around with visitors myself, which I should keep on doing now, only that my spirits make a little ease absolutely necessary. It's not a common offer, bear in mind," said the lady, rising into the tone and manner in which she was accustomed to address her audiences; "it's Jarley's wax-work, remember. The duty's very light and genteel, the company particularly select, the exhibition takes place in assembly-rooms, town halls, large rooms at inns, or auction galleries. There is none of your open-air wagrancy at Jarley's, recollect; there is no tarpaulin and sawdust at Jarley's, remember. Every expectation held out in the hand-bills is realized to the utmost, and the whole forms an effect of imposing brilliancy hitherto unrivaled in this kingdom. Remember that the price of admission is only sixpence, and that this is an opportunity which may never occur again!"

"We are very much obliged to you, ma'am," said Nell, "and thankfully accept your offer."

"And you'll never be sorry for it," returned Mrs. Jarley. "I'm pretty sure of that. So as that's all settled, let us have a bit of supper."

Rumbling along with most unwonted noise, the caravan stopped at last at the place of exhibition, where Nell dismounted amidst an admiring group of children, who evidently supposed her to be an important item of the curiosities, and were fully impressed with the belief that her grandfather was a cunning device in wax. The chests were taken out of the van for the figures with all convenient dispatch, and taken in to be unlocked by Mrs. Jarley, who, attended by George and the driver, disposed their contents (consisting of red festoons and other ornamental devices in upholstery work) to the best advantage in the decoration of the room.

When the festoons were all put up as tastily as they might be, the stupendous collection was uncovered, and there were displayed, on a raised platform some two feet from the floor, running round the room and parted from the rude public by a crimson rope, breast high, divers sprightly effigies of celebrated characters, singly and in groups, clad in glittering dresses of various climes and times and standing more or less unsteadily upon their legs, with their eyes very wide open, and their nostrils very much inflated, and the muscles of their legs and arms very strongly developed, and all their countenances expressing great surprise. All the gentlemen were very pigeon-breasted and very blue about the beards; and all the ladies were miraculous figures; and all

the ladies and all
the gentlemen were
looking intensely nowhere,
and staring with extraor-
dinary earnestness at noth
ing.

NELL AND HER GRANDFATHER IN
THE CHURCHYARD.

When Nell had exhausted her first raptures at this
glorious sight, Mrs. Jarley ordered the room to be cleared
of all but herself and the child, and sitting herself

down in an arm-chair in the centre, formally invested Nell
with a willow wand, long used by herself for pointing out
the characters, and was at great pains to instruct her in her
duty.

"That," said Mrs. Jarley, in her exhibition tone, as
Nell touched a figure at the beginning of the platform, "is
an unfortunate maid of honor in the time of Queen Elizabeth,
who died from pricking her finger in consequence of working
upon a Sunday.   Observe the blood which is trickling from
her finger; also the gold-eyed needle of the period, with
which she is at work."

All this Nell repeated twice or thrice,—pointing to the
finger and the needle at the right times; and then passed on
to the next.

"That, ladies and gentlemen," said Mrs. Jarley, "is
Jasper Packlemerton, of atrocious memory, who courted
and married fourteen wives, and destroyed them all, by
tickling the soles of their feet when they were sleeping in the
consciousness of innocence and virtue.   On being brought
to the scaffold and asked if he was sorry for what he had
done, he replied yes, he was sorry for having let 'em off so
easy, and hoped all Christian husbands would pardon him
the offense.   Let this be a warning to all young ladies to be
particular in the character of the gentlemen of their choice.
Observe that his fingers are curled as if in the act of tickling,
and that his face is represented with a wink, as he appeared
when committing his barbarous murders."

When Nell knew all abont Mr. Packlemerton, and
could say it without faltering, Mrs. Jarley passed on to the
fat man, and then to the thin man, the tall man, the short
man, the old lady who died of dancing at a hundred and
thirty-two, the wild boy of the woods, the woman who

poisoned fourteen families with pickled walnuts, and other historical characters and interesting but misguided individuals. And so well did Nell profit by her instructions, and so apt was she to remember them, that by the time they had been shut up together for a couple of hours, she was in full possession of the history of the whole establishment, and perfectly competent to the enlightenment of visitors.

For some time her life and the life of the poor vacant old man passed quietly and happily.

But heavier sorrow was yet to come. One night, a holiday night for them, Nell and her grandfather went out to walk. A terrible thunder-storm coming on, they were forced to take refuge in a small public house; and here some sinister and ill-favored men were playing cards. The old man watched them with increasing interest and excitement, until his whole appearance underwent a complete change. His face was flushed and eager, his teeth set. With a hand that trembled violently he seized Nell's little purse, and in spite of her entreaties joined in the game, gambling with such a savage thirst for gain that the distressed and frightened child could almost better have borne to see him dead. The night was far advanced before the play came to an end, and they were forced to remain where they were until the morning. And in the night the child was wakened from her troubled sleep to find a figure in the room—a figure busying its hands about her garments, while its face was turned to her, listening and looking lest she should awake. It was her grandfather himself, his white face pinched and sharpened by the greediness which made his eyes unnaturally bright, counting the money of which his hands were robbing her.

Evening after evening, after that night the old man

would steal away, not to return until the night was far spent, demanding, wildly, money. And at last there came an hour when the child overheard him, tempted beyond his feeble powers of resistance, undertake to find more money to feed the desperate passion which had laid its hold upon his weakness by robbing Mrs. Jarley.

That night the child took her grandfather by the hand and led him forth. Through the straight streets and narrow outskirts of the town their trembling feet passed quickly; the child sustained by one idea—that they were flying from disgrace and crime, and that her grandfather's preservation must depend solely upon her firmness unaided by one word of advice or any helping hand—the old man following her as though she had been an angel messenger sent to lead him where she would.

The hardest part of all their wanderings was now before them. They slept in the open air that night, and on the following morning some men offered to take them a long distance on their barge. These men, though they were not unkindly, were very rugged, noisy fellows, and they drank and quarreled fearfully among themselves, to Nell's inexpressible terror. It rained, too, heavily, and she was wet and cold. At last they reached the great city whither the barge was bound, and here they wandered up and down, being now penniless, and watched the faces of those who passed, to find among them a ray of encouragement or hope. Ill in body, and sick to death at heart, the child needed her utmost firmness and resolution even to creep along.

They laid down that night, and the next night too, with nothing between them and the sky; a penny loaf was all they had had that day, and when the third morning came, it found the child much weaker, yet she made no complaint.

The great manufacturing city hemmed them in on every side, and seemed to shut out hope.

Faint and spiritless as they were, its streets were insupportable. After humbly asking for relief at some few doors, and being repulsed, they agreed to make their way out of it as speedily as they could, and try if the inmates of any lone house beyond would have more pity on their exhausted state.

They were dragging themselves along through the last street, and the child felt that the time was close at hand when her enfeebled powers would bear no more. There appeared before them, at this juncture, going in the same direction as themselves, a traveler on foot, who, with a portmanteau strapped to his back, leaned upon a stout stick as he walked, and read from a book which he held in his other hand.

It was not an easy matter to come up with him and beseech his aid, for he walked fast, and was a little distance in advance. At length he stopped, to look more attentively at some passage in his book. Animated with a ray of hope, the child shot on before her grandfather, and, going close to to the stranger without rousing him by the sound of her footsteps, began, in a few faint words, to implore his help.

He turned his head. The child clapped her hands together, uttered a wild shriek and fell senseless at his feet.

It was the poor schoolmaster. No other than the poor schoolmaster. Scarcely less moved and surprised by the sight of the child than she had been on recognizing him, he stood, for a moment, silent, without even the presence of mind to raise her from the ground.

But, quickly recovering his self-possession, he threw down his stick and book, and dropping on one knee beside

her, endeavored. by such simple means as occurred to him,
to restore her to herself; while her grandfather, standing idly

"SHE WOULD STEAL INTO THE CHURCH AND SIT UPON THE TOMBS."

by, wrung his hands, and implored her, with many endear-
ing expressions, to speak to him, were it only a word.

"She appears to be quite exhausted," said the schoolmaster, glancing upward into his face. "You have taxed
her powers too far, friend."

"She is perishing of want," rejoined the old man. 'I never thought how weak and ill she was till now."

Casting a look upon him, half reproachful and half compassionate, the schoolmaster took the child in his arms, and bidding the old man gather up her little basket and follow him directly, bore her away at his utmost speed.

There was a small inn within sight, to which, it would seem, he had been directing his steps when so unexpectedly overtaken. Toward this place he hurried with his unconscious burden, and rushing into the kitchen, and calling upon the company there assembled to make way for God's sake, deposited it on a chair before the fire.

The company, who rose in confusion on the schoolmaster's entrance, did as people usually do under such circumstances. Everybody called for his or her favorite remedy, which nobody brought; each cried for more air, at the same time carefully excluding what air there was by closing around the object of sympathy; and all wondered why somebody else didn't do what it never appeared to occur to them might be done by themselves.

The landlady, however, who possessed more readiness and activity than any one of them, and who had withal a quicker perception of the merits of the case, soon came running in, with a little hot brandy-and-water, followed by her servant-girl, carrying vinegar, hartshorn, smelling-salts, and such other restoratives; which, being duly administered, recovered the child so far as to enable her to thank them in a faint voice, and to extend her hand to the poor schoolmaster, who stood, with an anxious face, hard by. Without suffering her to speak another word, or so much as to stir a finger any more, the women straightway carried her off to bed; and, having covered her up warm, bathed her cold feet, and wrapped them in flannel, they dispatched a messenger for the doctor.

The doctor, who was a red-nosed gentleman with a great bunch of seals dangling below a waist coat of ribbed black satin, arrived with all speed, and taking his seat by the bedside of poor Nell, drew out his watch, and felt her pulse. Then he looked at her tongue, then he felt her pulse again, and while he did so, he eyed the half-emptied wine-glass as if in profound abstraction.

"I should give her," said the doctor at length, "a teaspoonful, every now and then, of hot brandy-and-water."

"Why that's exactly what we've done, sir!" said the delighted landlady.

"I should also," observed the doctor, who had passed the foot-bath on the stairs, "I should also," said the doctor, in the voice of an oracle, "put her feet in hot water and wrap them up in flannel. I should likewise," said the doctor, with increased solemnity, "give her something light for supper—the wing of a roasted fowl now——"

"Why; goodness gracious me, sir, it's cooking at the kitchen fire this instant!" cried the landlady. And so, indeed, it was, for the school-master had ordered it to be put down, and it was getting on so well that the doctor might have smelled it if he had tried; perhaps he did.

"You may then," said the doctor, rising gravely, "give her a glass of hot mulled port-wine, if she likes wine——"

"And a toast, sir?" suggested the landlady.

"Ay," said the doctor, in the tone of a man who makes a dignified concession. "And a toast—of bread. But be very particular to make it of bread, if you please, ma'am."

With which parting injunction, slowly and portentously

delivered, the doctor departed, leaving the whole house in admiration of that wisdom which tallied so closely with their own. Everybody said he was a very shrewd doctor; indeed, and knew perfectly what people's constitutions were; which there appears some reason to suppose he did.

While her supper was preparing, the child fell into a refreshing sleep, from which they were obliged to rouse her when it was ready. As she evinced extraordinary uneasiness on learning that her grandfather was below stairs, and as she was greatly troubled at the thought of their being apart, he took his supper with her. Finding her still very restless on this head, they made him up a bed in an inner room, to which he presently retired. The key of this chamber happened by good-fortune to be on that side of the door which was in Nell's room; she turned it on him when the landlady had withdrawn, and crept to bed again with a thankful heart.

The schoolmaster sat for a long time smoking his pipe by the kitchen fire, which was now deserted; thinking, with a very happy face, on the fortunate chance which had brought him so opportunely to the child's assistance.

The schoolmaster, as it appeared, was on his way to a new home. And when the child had recovered somewhat from her exhaustion, it was arranged that she and her grandfather should accompany him to the village whither he was bound, and that he should endeavor to find them some humble occupation by which they could subsist.

It was a secluded village, lying among the quiet country scenes Nell loved. And here, her grandfather being tranquil and at rest, a great peace fell upon the spirit of the child. Often she would steal into the church, and, sitting down among the quiet figures carved upon the tombs, would think

of the summer days
spring-time t h a t
the rays of sun that
aslant those sleep-
songs of birds, and
w o u l d s t e a l i n.
awakened thoughts
would be no pain to
sights and
sounds as
t h e s e.
F o r t h e
time was
drawing

and the b r i g h t
would come; o f
w o u l d f a l l i n,
ing forms; of the
the sweet air that
What if the spot
o f d e a t h! I t
sleep amid such

DAY AFTER DAY THE OLD MAN WOULD SIT BESIDE HER GRAVE

nearer every day when Nell was to rest indeed. She never
murmured or complained, but faded like a light upon a
summer's evening and died. Day after day and all day
long, the old man, broken-hearted and with no love or care
for anything in life, would sit beside her grave with her
straw hat and the little basket she had been used to carry,
waiting till she should come to him again. At last they found
him lying dead upon the stone. And in the church where
they had often prayed and mused and lingered, hand in
hand, the child and the old man slept together.

Little Dorrit.

MANY years ago, when people could be put in prison for debt, a poor gentleman, who was unfortunate enough to lose all his money, was brought to the Marshalsea prison. As there seemed no prospect of being able to pay his debts, his wife and their two little children came to live there with him. The elder child was a boy of three; the younger a little girl of two years old, and not long afterwards another little girl was born. The three children played in the courtyard, and were happy on the whole, for they were too young to remember a happier state of things.

But the youngest child, who had never been outside the prison walls, was a thoughtful little creature, and wondered what the outside world could be like. Her great friend, the turnkey, who was also her godfather, became very fond of her, and as soon as she could walk and talk he bought a little arm-chair and stood it by his fire at the lodge, and coaxed her with cheap toys to come and sit with him. In return the child loved him dearly, and would often bring her doll to dress and undress as she sat in the little arm-chair. She was still a very tiny creature when she began to understand that everyone did not live locked up inside high walls with spikes at the top, and though she and the rest of the family might pass through the door that the great key opened, her father could not; and she would look at him with a wondering pity in her tender little heart.

One day, she was sitting in the lodge gazing wistfully up at the sky through the barred window. The turnkey, after watching her some time, said:

"Thinking of the fields, ain't you?"

"Where are they?" she asked.

"Why, they're—over there, my dear," said the turnkey, waving his key vaguely, "just about there."

"Does anybody open them and shut them? Are they locked?"

"Well," said the turnkey, discomfited, "not in general."

"Are they pretty, Bob?" She called him Bob, because he wished it.

"Lovely. Full of flowers. There's buttercups and there's daisies, and there's—" here he hesitated, not knowing the names of many flowers—"there's dandelions, and all manner of games."

"Is it very pleasant to be there, Bob?"

"Prime," said the turnkey.

"Was father ever there?"

"Hem!" coughed the turnkey. "Oh, yes, he was there, sometimes."

"Is he sorry not to be there now?"

"N—not particular," said the turnkey.

"Nor any of the people?" she asked, glancing at the listless crowd within. "Oh, are you quite sure and certain, Bob?"

At this point, Bob gave in and changed the subject to hardbake. But after this chat the turnkey and little Amy would go out on his free Sunday afternoons to some meadows or green lanes, and she would pick grass and flowers to bring home, while he smoked his pipe; and then they would go to some tea-gardens for shrimps and tea and other delicacies, and would come back hand in hand, unless she was very tired and had fallen asleep on his shoulder.

When Amy was only eight years old her mother died,

4

"THINKING OF THE FIELDS, AIN'T YOU?"

and the poor father was more helpless and broken-down
than ever, and as Fanny was a careless child, and Edward
idle, the little one, who had the bravest and truest heart, was
inspired by her love and unselfishness to be the little mother
of the forlorn family, and struggled to get some little education for herself and her brother and sister.

At first, such a baby could do little more than sit with
him, deserting her livelier place by the high fender, and
quietly watching him. But this made her so far necessary
to him that he became accustomed to her, and began to be
sensible of missing her when she was not there. Through
this little gate, she passed out of her childhood into the
care-laden world.

What her pitiful look saw, at that early time, in her father,
in her sister, in her brother, in the jail; how much or how
little of the wretched truth it pleased God to make visible to
her, lies hidden with many mysteries. It is enough that she
was inspired to be something which was not what the rest
were, and to be that something, different and laborious, for
for the sake of the rest. Inspired? Yes. Shall we speak
of the inspiration of a poet or a priest, and not of the heart
impelled by love and self-devotion to the lowliest work in
the lowliest way of life?

At thirteen she could read and keep accounts—that is,
could put down in words and figures how much the bare
necessaries that they wanted would cost, and how much less
they had to buy them with. She had been, by snatches of a
few weeks at a time, to an evening school outside, and got
her sister and brother sent to day-school by desultory starts,
during three or four years. There was no instruction for
any of them at home; but she knew well—no one better—
that a man so broken as to be the Father of the Marshalsea,
could be no father to his own children.

To these scanty means of improvement, she added another of her own contriving. Once among the crowd of inmates there appeared a dancing-master. Her sister had a great desire to learn the dancing-master's art, and seemed to have a taste that way. At thirteen years old, the Child of the Marshalsea presented herself to the dancing-master, with a little bag in her hand, and offered her humble petition.

"If you please, I was born here, sir."

"Oh! You are the young lady, are you?" said the dancing-master, surveying the small figure and uplifted face.

"Yes, sir."

"And what can I do for you?" said the dancing-master.

"Nothing for me, sir, thank you," anxiously undrawing the strings of the little bag, "but if, while you stay here, you could be so kind as to teach my sister cheap——"

"My child, I'll teach her for nothing," said the dancing-master, shutting up the bag. He was as good-natured a dancing-master as ever danced to the Insolvent Court, and he kept his word. The sister was so apt a pupil, and the dancing-master had such abundant leisure to bestow upon her, that wonderful progress was made. Indeed, the dancing-master was so proud of it, and so wishful to display it before he left, to a few select friends among the collegians, that at six o'clock on a certain fine morning, a minuet de la cour came off in the yard—the college-rooms being of too confined proportions for the purpose—in which so much ground was covered, and the steps were so conscientiously executed, that the dancing-master, having to play the kit besides, was thoroughly blown.

The success of this beginning, which led to the dancing-master's continuing his instruction after his release, emboldened the poor child to try again. She watched and waited months for a seamstress. In the fullness of time a milliner came in, and to her she repaired on her own behalf.

"I beg your pardon, ma'am," she said, looking timidly round the door of the milliner, whom she found in tears and in bed, "but I was born here."

Everybody seemed to hear of her as soon as they arrived; for the milliner sat up in bed, drying her eyes, and said, just as the dancing-master had said:

"Oh! *You* are the child, are you?"

"Yes, ma'am."

"I am sorry I haven't got anything for you," said the milliner, shaking her head.

"It's not that, ma'am. If you please, I want to learn needlework."

"Why should you do that," returned the milliner, "with me before you? It has not done me much good."

"Nothing—whatever it is—seems to have done anybody much good who comes here," she returned in all simplicity, "but I want to learn, just the same."

"I am afraid you are so weak, you see," the milliner objected.

"I don't think I am weak, ma'am."

"And you are so very, very little, you see," the milliner objected.

"Yes, I am afraid I am very little indeed," returned the Child of the Marshalsea; and so began to sob over that unfortunate defect of hers, which came so often in her way.

The milliner—who was not morose or hard-hearted, only newly insolvent—was touched, took her in hand with good-will, found her the most patient and earnest of pupils, and made her a good workwoman.

In the course of time, the Father of the Marshalsea gradually developed a new flower of character. With the same hand that had pocketed a collegian's half-crown half an hour ago, he would wipe away the tears that streamed over his cheeks if any reference were made to his daughters' earning their bread. So, over and above her other daily cares, the Child of the Marshalsea had always upon her the care of preserving the genteel fiction that they were all idle beggars together.

The sister became a dancer. There was a ruined uncle in the family group—ruined by his brother, the father of the Marshalsea, and knowing no more how than his ruiner did, but accepting the fact as an inevitable certainty. Naturally a retired and simple man, he had shown no particular sense of being ruined at the time when that calamity fell upon him, further than he left off washing himself when the shock was announced, and never took that luxury any more. He had been a very indifferent musical amateur in his better days; and when he fell with his brother, resorted for support to playing a clarionet as dirty as himself in a small theatre orchestra. It was the theatre in which his niece became a dancer; he had been a fixture there a long time when she took her poor station in it, and he accepted the task of serving as her escort and guardian, just as he would have accepted an illness, a legacy, a feast, starvation—anything but soap.

To enable this girl to earn her few weekly shillings, it was necessary for the Child of the Marshalsea to go through an elaborate form with her father.

"Fanny is not going to live with us, just now, father. She will be here a good deal in the day, but she is going to live outside with uncle."

"You surprise me! Why?"

"I think uncle wants a companion, father. He should be attended to and looked after."

"A companion? He passes much of his time here. And you attend and look after him, Amy, a great deal more than ever your sister will. You all go out so much; you all go out so much!"

This was to keep up the ceremony and pretense of his having no idea that Amy herself went out by the day to work.

"But we are always very glad to come home, father; now, are we not? And as to Fanny, perhaps besides keeping uncle company and taking care of him, it may be as well for her not quite to live here always. She was not born here as I was you know, father.

"Well, Amy, well. I don't quite follow you, but it's natural, I suppose, that Fanny should prefer to be outside, and even that you often should, too. So you and Fanny and your uncle, my dear, shall have your own way. Good, good. I'll not meddle; don't mind me."

To get her brother out of prison—out of the succession to Mrs. Bangham in executing commissions, and out of the slang interchange with very doubtful companions, consequent upon both, was her hardest task. At eighteen he would have dragged on from hand to mouth, from hour to hour, from penny to penny, until eighty. Nobody got into the prison from whom he derived anything useful or good, and she could find no patron for him but her old friend and godfather.

"Dear Bob," said she, "what is to become of poor Tip?" His name was Edward, and Ted had been transformed into Tip, within the walls.

The turnkey had strong private opinions as to what would become of poor Tip, and had even gone so far with the view of averting their fulfillment as to sound Tip in reference to the expediency of running away and going to serve his country. But Tip had thanked him, and said he didn't seem to care for his country.

"Well, my dear," said the turnkey, "something ought to be done with him. Suppose I try and get him into the law?"

"That would be so good of you, Bob!"

The turnkey had now two points to put to the professional gentlemen as they passed in and out. He put this second one so perseveringly that a stool and twelve shillings a week were at last found for Tip in the office of an attorney in a great National Palladium called the Palace Court; at that time one of a considerable list of everlasting bulwarks to the dignity and safety of Albion, whose places know them no more.

Tip languished in Clifford's Inn for six months, and at the expiration of that term sauntered back one evening with his hands in his pockets, and incidentally observed to his sister that he was not going back again.

"Not going back again?" said the poor little anxious Child of the Marshalsea, always calculating and planning for Tip, in the front rank of her charges.

"I am so tired of it," said Tip, "that I have cut it."

Tip tired of everything. With intervals of Marshalsea lounging, and Mrs. Bangham succession, his small second mother, aided by her trusty friend, got him into a warehouse, into a market garden, into the hop trade, into the law again, into an auctioneer's, into a brewery, into a stockbroker's, into the law again, into a coach office, into a wagon office, into the law again, into a general dealer's, into a distillery, into

LITTLE DORRIT AND MAGGIE

the law again, into a wool house, into a dry goods house, into the Billingsgate trade, into the foreign fruit trade, and into the docks. But whatever Tip went into he came out of tired, announcing that he had cut it. Wherever he went, this foredoomed Tip appeared to take the prison walls with him, and to set them up in such trade or calling; and to prowl about within their narrow limits in the old slipshod, purposeless, down-at-heel way; until the real, immovable Marshalsea walls asserted their fascination over him and brought him back.

Nevertheless, the brave little creature did so fix her heart on her brother's rescue that, while he was ringing out these doleful changes, she pinched and scraped enough together to ship him for Canada. When he was tired of nothing to do, and disposed in its turn to cut even that, he graciously consented to go to Canada. And there was grief in her bosom over parting with him, and joy in the hope of being put in a straight course at last.

"God bless you, dear Tip. Don't be too proud to come and see us, when you have made your fortune."

"All right!" said Tip, and went.

But not all the way to Canada; in fact, not further than Liverpool. After making the voyage to that port from London, he found himself so strongly impelled to cut the vessel that he resolved to walk back again. Carrying out which intention, he presented himself before her at the expiration of a month, in rags, without shoes, and much more tired than ever.

At length, after another interval of successorship to Mrs. Bangham, he found a pursuit for himself, and announced it.

"Amy, I have got a situation."

"Have you, really and truly, Tip?"

"All right. I shall do now. You needn't look anxious about me any more, old girl."

"What is it, Tip?"

"Why, you know Slingo by sight?"

"Not the man they call the dealer?

TIP AND LITTLE DORRIT.
" Don't say that you are a prisoner, Tip !"

"That's the chap. He'll be out on Monday, and he's going to give me a berth."

"What is he a dealer in, Tip?"

"Horses. All right! I shall do now, Amy."

She lost sight of him for months afterwards, and only heard from him once. A whisper passed among the elder collegians that he had been seen at a mock auction in Moorfields, pretending to buy plated articles for massive silver, and paying for them with the greatest liberality in bank-notes; but it never reached her ear. One evening she was alone at work—standing up at the window, to save the twilight lingering above the wall—when he opened the door and walked in.

She kissed him and welcomed him; but was afraid to ask him any question. He saw how anxious and timid she was, and appeared sorry.

"I am afraid, Amy, you'll be vexed this time. Upon my life I am!"

"I am very sorry to hear you say so, Tip. Have you come back?"

"Why—yes."

"Not expecting this time that what you had found would answer very well, I am less surprised and sorry than I might have been, Tip."

"Ah! But that's not the worst of it."

"Not the worst of it?"

"Don't look so startled. No, Amy, not the worst of it. I have come back, you see; but—*don't* look so startled—I have come back in what I may call a new way. I am off the volunteer list altogether. I am in now as one of the regulars."

"Oh! Don't say that you are a prisoner, Tip! Don't, don't"

"Well, I don't want to say it," he returned in a reluctant tone; "but if you can't understand me without my saying it, what am I to do? I am in for forty pound odd."

For the first time in all those years, she sunk under her cares. She cried, with her clasped hands lifted above her head, that it would kill their father if he ever knew it; and fell down at Tip's graceless feet.

It was easier for Tip to bring her to her senses than for her to bring *him* to understand that the Father of the Marshalsea would be beside himself if he knew the truth. The thing was incomprehensible to Tip and altogether a fanciful notion. He yielded to it in that light only when he submitted to her entreaties, backed by those of his uncle and sister. There was no want of precedent for his return; it was accounted for to the father in the usual way, and the collegians, with a better comprehension of the pious fraud than Tip, supported it loyally.

This was the life, and this the history, of the child of the Marshalsea, at twenty-two. With a still surviving attachment to the one miserable yard and block of houses as her birthplace and home, she passed to and fro in it shrinkingly now, with a womanly consciousness that she was pointed out to everyone. Since she had begun to work beyond the walls, she had found it necessary to conceal where she lived, and to come and go as secretly as she could between the free city and the iron gates, outside of which she had never slept in her life. Her original timidity had grown with this concealment, and her light step and her little figure shunned the thronged streets while they passed along them.

Worldly wise in hard and poor necessities, she was innocent in all things else. Innocent in the mist through which she saw her father and the prison and the turbid living river that flowed through it and flowed on.

This was the life, and this the history, of little Dorrit, until the son of a lady, Mrs. Clennem, to whose house Amy went to do needlework, became interested in the pale, patient little creature, and learning her history resolved to do his best to try to get her father released, and to help them all.

One day when he was walking home with Amy to try
to find out the names of some of the people her father owed
money to, a voice was heard calling, "Little mother, little
mother," and a strange
figure came bouncing
up to them and fell
down, scattering her
basketful of potatoes
on the ground. "Oh
Maggie," said Amy,
"what a clumsy child
you are!"

She was about
eight and twenty, with
large bones, large fea-
tures, large hands and
feet, large eyes, and
no hair. Amy told
Mr. Clennem that
Maggie was the grand-
daughter of her old
nurse, who had been
dead a long time, and
that her grandmother
had been very unkind
to her and beat her.

MAGGIE.
"Oh, ain't it a delightful place to stop at!"

"When Maggie was ten years old she had a fever, and
she has never grown older since."

"Ten years old," said Maggie. "But what a nice
hospital! So comfortable, wasn't it? Such a 'e'v'nly place!
Such beds there is there! Such lemonades! Such oranges!
Such delicious broth and wine! Such chicking! Oh, ain't
it a delightful place to stop at!"

"Then when she came out, her grandmother did not know what to do with her, and was very unkind. But after some time Maggie tried to improve, and was very attentive and industrious, and now she can earn her own living entirely, sir!"

Amy did not say who had taken pains to teach and encourage the poor, half-witted creature, but Mr. Clennem guessed from the name little mother and the fondness of the poor creature for Amy.

One cold, wet evening, Amy and Maggie went to Mr. Clennem's house to thank him for having freed Edward from the prison, and on coming out found it was too late to get home as the gate was locked. They tried to get in at Maggie's lodgings, but, though they knocked twice, the people were asleep. As Amy did not wish to disturb them, they wandered about all night, sometimes sitting at the gate of the prison, Maggie shivering and whimpering.

"It will soon be over, dear," said patient Amy.

"Oh, it's all very well for you, mother," said Maggie, "but I'm a poor thing, only ten years old."

Thanks to Mr. Clennem, a great change took place in the fortunes of the family, and not long after this wretched night it was discovered that Mr. Dorrit was owner of a large property, and they became very rich.

But little Dorrit never forgot, as, sad to say, the rest of the family did, the friends who had been kind to them in their poverty; and when in his turn, Mr. Clennem became a prisoner in the Marshalsea, Little Dorrit came to comfort and console him, and after many changes of fortune she became his wife, and they lived happy ever after.

Trotty Veck and His Daughter Meg.

"TROTTY" seems a strange name for an old man, but it was given to Toby Veck because of his always going at a trot to do his errands; for he was a ticket porter, and his office was to take letters and messages for people who were in too great a hurry to send them by the post, which in those days was neither so cheap nor so quick as it is now. He did not earn very much, and had to be out in all weathers and all day long. But Toby was of a cheerful disposition, and looked on the bright side of everything, and was grateful for any small mercies that came in his way;

and so was happier than many people who never knew what it was to be hungry or in want of comforts. His greatest joy was his dear, bright, pretty daughter Meg, who loved him dearly.

One cold day, near the end of the year, Toby had been waiting a long time for a job, trotting up and down in his usual place before the church, and trying hard to keep himself warm, when the bells chimed twelve o'clock, which made Toby think of dinner.

"There's nothing," he remarked, carefully feeling his nose to make sure it was still there, "more regular in coming round than dinner-time, and nothing less regular in coming round than dinner.   That's the great difference between 'em." He went on talking to himself, trotting up and down, and never noticing who was coming near to him.

"Why, father, father," said a pleasant voice, and Toby turned to find his daughter's sweet, bright eyes close to his.

"Why pet," said he, kissing her and squeezing her blooming face between his hands, "what's to-do? I didn't expect you to-day, Meg."

"Neither did I expect to come, father," said Meg, nodding and smiling. "But here I am! And not alone, not alone!"

"Why, you don't mean to say," observed Trotty, looking curiously at the covered basket she carried, "that you—"

"Smell it, father dear," said Meg. "Only smell it!"

Trotty was going to lift up the cover at once, in a great hurry, when she gaily interposed her hand.

"No, no, no," said Meg, with the glee of a child. "Lengthen it out a little.   Let me just lift up the corner; just a lit-tle, ti-ny cor-ner, you know," said Meg, suiting the action to the word with the utmost gentleness, and speaking

very softly, as if she were afraid of being overheard by
something inside the basket.   "There, now; what's that?"

Toby took the shortest possible sniff at the edge of the
basket, and cried out in rapture:

"Why, it's hot," he said.

"THEY BROKE IN LIKE A GRACE, MY DEAR."

But to Meg's great delight he could not guess what it
was that smelt so good.

"Polonies? Trotters? Liver? Pettitoes? Sausages?" he
tried one after the other.   At last he exclaimed in triumph.
"Why, what am I a'thinking of?   It's tripe!"

And it was.

"And so," said Meg, "I'll lay the cloth at once, father;
for I have brought the tripe in a basin, and tied the basin

5

up in a pocket-handkerchief; and if I like to be proud for once, and spread that for a cloth, and call it a cloth, there's nobody to prevent me, is there, father?"

"Not that I know of, my dear," said Toby; "but they're always a-bringing up some new law or other."

"And according to what I was reading you in the paper, the other day, father, what the judge said, you know, we poor people are supposed to know them all.   Ha, ha! What a mistake!   My goodness me, how clever they think us!"

"Yes, my dear," cried Trotty; "and they'd be very fond of any one of us that *did* know 'em all. He'd grow fat upon the work he'd get, that man, and be popular with the gentlefolks in his neighborhood.   Very much so!"

"He'd eat his dinner with an appetite, whoever he was, if it smelt like this," said Meg, cheerfully.   "Make haste, for there's a hot potato besides, and half a pint of fresh-drawn beer in a bottle.   Where will you dine, father—on the post or on the steps?   Dear, dear, how grand we are! Two places to choose from!"

"The steps to-day, my pet," said Trotty.   "Steps in dry weather, post in wet.   There's greater conveniency in the steps at all times, because of the sitting down, but they're rheumatic in the damp."

"Then, here," said Meg, clapping her hands after a moment's bustle; "here it is all ready!   And beautiful it looks!   Come, father.   Come!"

And just as Toby was about to sit down to his dinner on the doorsteps of a big house close by, the chimes rang out again, and Toby took off his hat and said, "Amen."

"Amen to the bells, father?"

"They broke in like a grace, my dear," said Trotty;

"they'd say a good one if they could, I'm sure. Many's
the kind thing they say to me. How often have I heard
them bells say, 'Toby Veck, Toby Veck, keep a good heart,
Toby!' A million times? More!"

"Well, I never!" cried Meg.

"When things is very bad, then it's 'Toby Veck, Toby
Veck, job coming soon, Toby!'"

"And it comes—at last, father," said Meg, with a touch
of sadness in her pleasant voice.

"Always," answered Toby. "Never fails."

While this discourse was holding, Trotty made no
pause in his attack upon the savory meat before him, but
cut and ate, and cut and drank, and cut and chewed, and
dodged about from tripe to hot potato, and from hot potato
back again to tripe, with an unctuous and unflagging relish.
But happening now to look all round the street—in case anybody should be beckoning from any door or window for a
porter—his eyes in coming back again encountered Meg
sitting opposite him with her arms folded, and only busy
in watching his progress with a smile of happiness.

"Why, Lord forgive me!" said Trotty, dropping his
knife and fork. "My dove! Meg, why didn't you tell me
what a beast I was?"

"Father?"

"Sitting here," said Trotty, in penitent explanation,
"cramming and stuffing and gorging myself, and you
before me there, never so much as breaking your precious
fast, nor wanting to, when——"

"But I have broken it, father," interposed his daughter,
laughing, "all to bits. I have had my dinner."

"Nonsense," said Trotty. "Two dinners in one day!
It ain't possible! You might as well tell me that two New

Year's days will come together, or that I have had a gold head all my life, and never changed it."

"I have had my dinner, father, for all that," said Meg, coming nearer to him. "And if you will go on with yours, I'll tell you how and where, and how your dinner came to be (brought, and—and something else besides."

Toby still appeared incredulous; but she looked into his face with her clear eyes, and, laying her hand upon his shoulder, motioned him to go on while the meat was hot. So Trotty took up his knife and fork again and went to work, but much more slowly than before, and shaking his head, as if he were not at all pleased with himself.

"I had my dinner, father," said Meg, after a little hesitation, "with—with Richard. His dinner-time was early; and as he brought his dinner with him when he came to see me, we—we had it together, father."

Trotty took a little beer and smacked his lips. Then he said "Oh!" because she waited.

"And Richard says, father—" Meg resumed, then stopped.

"What does Richard say, Meg?" asked Toby.

"Richard says, father—" Another stoppage.

"Richard's a long time saying it," said Toby.

"He says, then, father," Meg continued, lifting up her eyes at last, and speaking in a tremble, but quite plainly, "another year is nearly gone, and where is the use of waiting on from year to year, when it is so unlikely we shall ever be better off than we are now? He says we are poor now, father, and we shall be poor then; but we are young now, and years will make us old before we know it. He says that if we wait, people in our condition, until we see our way quite clearly, the way will be a narrow one indeed—the common way—the grave, father."

TROTTY VECK'S DINNER

A bolder man than Trotty Veck must needs have drawn upon his boldness largely to deny it. Trotty held his peace.

"And how hard, father, to grow old and die, and think we might have cheered and helped each other! How hard in all our lives to love each other, and to grieve, apart, to see each other working, changing, growing old and gray. Even if I got the better of it, and forgot him (which I never could), oh, father, dear, how hard to have a heart so full as mine is now, and live to have it slowly drained out every drop, without the recollection of one happy moment of a woman's life to stay behind and comfort me and make me better!"

Trotty sat quite still. Meg dried her eyes, and said more gaily—that is to say, with here a laugh and there a sob, and here a laugh and sob together:

"So Richard says, father, as his work was yesterday made certain for some time to come, and as I love him and have loved him full three years—ah, longer than that, if he knew it!—will I marry him on New Year's Day?"

Just then Richard himself came up to persuade Toby to agree to their plan and, almost at the same moment, a footman came out of the house and ordered them all off the steps, and some gentleman came out who called up Trotty, and asked a great many questions, and found a good deal of fault, telling Richard he was very foolish to want to get married, which made Toby feel very unhappy and Richard very angry. So the lovers went off together, sadly; Richard looking gloomy and downcast, and Meg in tears. Toby, who had a letter given him to carry, and a sixpence, trotted off in rather low spirits to a very grand house, where he was told to take the letter in to the gentleman. While waiting he heard the letter read. It was from Alderman Cute, to tell Sir Joseph Bowley that one of his tenants named Will Fern,

who had come to London to try to get work, had been
brought before him charged with sleeping in a shed, and
asking if Sir Joseph wished him to be dealt leniently
with or otherwise. To Toby's great disappointment, for Sir
Joseph had talked a great deal about being a friend to the
poor, the answer was given that Will Fern might be sent to
prison as a vagabond, and made an example of, though his
only fault was poverty. On his way home, Toby, thinking
sadly, with his hat pulled down low on his head, ran against
a man dressed as a countryman, carrying a fair-haired little
girl. Toby inquired anxiously if he had hurt either of them.
The man answered no, and seeing Toby had a kind face, he
asked him the way to Alderman Cute's house.

"It's impossible," cried Toby, "that your name is Will
Fern?"

"That's my name," said the man.

Thereupon Toby told him what he had just heard, and
said, "Don't go there."

Poor Will told him how he could not make a living in
the country, and had come to London with his orphan niece to
try to find a friend of her mother's and to endeavor to get
some work, and, wishing Toby a happy New Year, was about
to trudge wearily off again, when Trotty caught his hand
saying:

"Stay! The New Year never can be happy to me if I see
the child and you go wandering away without a shelter for
your heads. Come home with me. I'm a poor man, living in
a poor place; but I can give you lodging for one night, and
never miss it. Come home with me! Here! I'll take her!"
cried Trotty, liftng up the child. "A pretty one! I'd carry
twenty times her weight and never know I'd got it. Tell me
if I go too quick for you. I'm very fast. I always was!"

Trotty said this taking about six of his trotting paces to one
stride of his fatigued companion, and with his thin legs quiv-
ering again beneath the load he bore.

"Why, she's as light," said Trotty, trotting in his speech
as well as in his gait—for he couldn't bear to be thanked, and
dreaded a moment's pause—"as light as a feather. Lighter
than a peacock's feather—a great deal lighter. Here we are
and here we go!" And, rushing in, he set the child down before
his daughter. The little girl gave one look at Meg's sweet
face and ran into her arms at once, while Trotty ran around
the room saying, "Here we are and here we go! Here, Uncle
Will, come to the fire. Meg, my precious darling, where's the
kettle? Here it is and here it goes, and it'll bile in no time!"

"Why, father!" said Meg, as she knelt before the child
and pulled off her wet shoes, "you're crazy to-night, I think.
I don't know what the bells would say to that. Poor little
feet, how cold they are!"

"Oh, they're warmer now!" exclaimed the child.
"They're quite warm now!"

"No, no, no," said Meg. "We haven't rubbed 'em half
enough. We're so busy. And when they're done we'll brush
out the damp hair; and when that's done we'll bring some
color to the poor, pale face with fresh water; and when that's
done we'll be so gay and happy!"

The child, sobbing, clasped her round the neck, saying,
"O Meg, O dear Meg!"

"Good gracious me!" said Meg presently, "father's
crazy. He's put the dear child's bonnet on the kettle, and
hung the lid behind the door!"

Trotty hastily repaired this mistake, and went off to find
some tea and a rasher of bacon he fancied "he had seen lying
somewhere on the stairs."

He soon came back and made the tea, and before long they were all enjoying a meal.   Trotty and Meg only took a morsel for form's sake, but their delight was in seeing their visitors eat, and very happy they were—though Trotty had noticed that Meg was sitting by the fire in tears when they had come in, and he feared her marriage had been broken off.

After tea Meg took Lilian to bed, and Toby showed Will Fern where he was to sleep.   As he came back past Meg's door he heard the child saying her prayers, remembering Meg's name and asking for his.   Then he went to sit by the fire and read his paper, and fell asleep to have a wonderful dream, so terrible and sad that it was a great relief when he woke.

"And whatever you do, father," said Meg, "don't eat tripe again without asking some doctor whether it's likely to agree with you; for how you *have* been going on!   Good gracious!"

She was working with her needle at a little table by the fire, dressing her simple gown with ribbons for her wedding— so quietly happy, so blooming and youthful, so full of beautiful promise, that he uttered a great cry as if it were an angel in his house, then flew to clasp her in his arms,

But he caught his feet in the newspaper, which had fallen on the hearth, and somebody came rushing in between them.

"No!" cried the voice of this same somebody.   A generous and jolly voice it was!   "Not even you; not even you.   The first kiss of Meg in the New Year is mine—mine! I have been waiting outside the house this hour to hear the bells and claim it.   Meg, my precious prize, a happy year! A life of happy years, my darling wife!"

And Richard smothered her with kisses.

You never in all your life saw anything like Trotty after this; I don't care where you have lived or what you have seen; you never in your life saw anything at all approaching him! He kept running up to Meg, and squeezing her fresh face between his hands and kissing it, going from her backwards not to lose sight of it, and running up again like a figure in a magic lantern; and whatever he did, he was constantly sitting himself down in his chair, and never stopping in it for one single moment, being—that's the truth—beside himself with joy.

"And to-morrow's your wedding-day, my pet!" cried Trotty. "Your real, happy wedding-day!"

"To-day!" cried Richard, shaking hands with him. "To-day. The chimes are ringing in the New Year. Hear them!"

They *were* ringing. Bless their sturdy hearts, they *were* ringing. Great bells as they were—melodious, deep-mouthed, noble bells, cast in no common metal, made by no common founder—when had they ever chimed like that before?

Trotty was backing off to that extraordinary chair again, when the child, who had been awakened by the noise, came running in, half-dressed.

"Why, here she is!" cried Trotty, catching her up. "Here's little Lilian! Ha, ha, ha! Here we are and here we go! Oh, here we are and here we go again! And here we are and here we go! And Uncle Will, too!"

Before Will Fern could make the least reply, a band of music burst into the room, attended by a flock of neighbors, screaming, "A Happy New Year, Meg!" "A happy wedding!" "Many of 'em!" and other fragmentary good-wishes of that sort. The Drum (who was a private friend of Trotty's) then stepped forward and said:

"Trotty Veck, my boy, it's got about that your daughter is going to be married to-morrow. There ain't a soul that knows you that don't wish you well, or that knows her and don't wish her well. Or that knows you both and don't wish you both all the happiness the New Year can bring. And here we are to play it in and dance it in accordingly."

Then Mrs. Chickenstalker came in (a good-humored, comely woman who, to the delight of all, turned out to be the friend of Lilian's mother, for whom Will Fern had come to look), with a stone pitcher full of "flip," to wish Meg joy, and then the music struck up, and Trotty, making Meg and Richard second couple, led off Mrs. Chickenstalker down the dance, and danced it in a step unknown before or since, founded on his own peculiar trot.

Tiny Tim.

IT will surprise you all very much to hear that there was once a man who did not like Christmas. In fact, he had been heard on several occasions to use the word *humbug* with regard to it. His name was Scrooge, and he was a hard, sour-tempered man of business, intent only on saving and making money, and caring nothing for anyone. He paid the poor, hard-working clerk in his office as little as he could possibly get the work done for, and lived on as little as possible himself, alone, in two dismal rooms. He was never merry or comfortable or happy, and he hated other people to be so, and that was the reason why he hated Christmas, because

BOB CRATCHIT AND TINY TIM

people *will* be happy at Christmas, you know, if they possibly can, and like to have a little money to make themselves and others comfortable.

Well, it was Christmas eve, a very cold and foggy one, and Mr. Scrooge, having given his poor clerk unwilling permission to spend Christmas day at home, locked up his office and went home himself in a very bad temper, and with a cold in his head. After having taken some gruel, as he

sat over a miserable fire in his dismal room, he got into bed
and had some wonderful and disagreeable dreams, to which
we will leave him, whilst we see how Tiny Tim, the son of
his poor clerk, spent Christmas day.

The name of this clerk was Bob Cratchit. He had a
wife and five other children besides Tim, who was a weak
and delicate little cripple, and for this reason was dearly
loved by his father and the rest of the family; not but what
he was a dear little boy, too, gentle and patient and loving,
with a sweet face of his own, which no one could help
looking at.

Whenever he could spare the time, it was Mr. Cratchit's
delight to carry his little boy out on his shoulder to see the
shops and the people; and to-day he had taken him to
church for the first time.

"Whatever has got your precious father and your
brother Tiny Tim!" exclaimed Mrs. Cratchit, "here's dinner
all ready to be dished up. I've never known him so late on
Christmas day before."

"Here he is, mother!" cried Belinda, and "here he is!"
cried the other children.

In came little Bob, the father, with at least three feet of
comforter, exclusive of the fringe, hanging down before
him; and his threadbare clothes darned up and brushed, to
look seasonable; and Tiny Tim upon his shoulder. Alas
for Tiny Tim, he bore a little crutch, and had his limbs supported by an iron frame!

"Why, where's our Martha?" cried Bob Cratchit,
looking round.

"Not coming," said Mrs. Cratchit.

"Not coming!" said Bob, with a sudden declension in
his high spirits; for he had been Tim's blood horse all the

way from church, and had come home rampant. "Not coming upon Christmas day!"

Martha didn't like to see him disappointed, if it were only in joke; so she came out prematurely from behind the closet-door, and ran into his arms, while the two young Cratchits hustled Tiny Tim, and bore him off into the wash-house, that he might hear the pudding singing in the copper.

"And how did Tim behave?" asked Mrs. Cratchit.

"As good as gold and better," replied his father. "I think, wife, the child gets thoughtful, sitting at home so much. He told me, coming home, that he hoped the people in church who saw he was a cripple would be pleased to remember on Christmas day who it was made the lame to walk."

"Bless his sweet heart!" said the mother in a trembling voice, and the father's voice trembled, too, as he remarked that "Tiny Tim was growing strong and hearty at last.

His active little crutch was heard upon the floor, and back came Tiny Tim before another word was spoken, escorted by his brother and sister to his stool beside the fire; while Bob, Master Peter, and the two ubiquitous young Cratchits went to fetch the goose, with which they soon returned in high procession.

Such a bustle ensued that you might have thought a goose the rarest of all birds; a feathered phenomenon, to which a black swan was a matter of course—and in truth it was something very like it in that house. Mrs. Cratchit made the gravy (ready beforehand in a little saucepan) hissing hot; Master Peter mashed the potatoes with incredible vigor; Miss Belinda sweetened up the apple-sauce; Martha dusted the hot plates; Bob took Tiny Tim beside him in a tiny corner at the table; the two young Cratchits set chairs for everybody, not forgetting themselves, and, mounting guard upon their posts, crammed spoons into their mouths, lest they should shriek for goose before their turn came to be helped. At last the dishes were set on, and grace was said. It was succeeded by a breathless pause, as Mrs. Cratchit, looking slowly all along the carving-knife, prepared to plunge it in the breast; but when she did, and when the long-expected gush of stuffing issued forth, one murmur of delight arose all round the board, and even Tiny Tim, excited by the two young Cratchits, beat on the table with the handle of his knife, and feebly cried, Hurrah!

There never was such a goose. Bob said he didn't believe there ever was such a goose cooked. Its tenderness and flavor, size and cheapness were the themes of universal admiration. Eked out by apple-sauce and mashed potatoes, it was a sufficient dinner for the whole family; indeed, as Mrs. Cratchit said with great delight (surveying one small atom of a bone upon the dish), they hadn't ate it all, at that! Yet everyone had had enough, and the youngest Cratchits, in particular, were steeped in sage and onions to the eyebrows! But now, the plates being changed by Miss Belinda, Mrs. Cratchit left the room alone—too nervous to bear witness—to take the pudding up, and bring it in.

Suppose it should not be done enough! Suppose it should break in turning out! Suppose somebody should have got over the wall of the back yard and stolen it, while they were merry with the goose—a supposition at which the two young Cratchits became livid! All sorts of horrors were supposed.

Halloo! A great deal of steam! The pudding was out of the copper. A smell like a washing-day! That was the cloth. A smell like an eating-house and a pastry cook's next door to each other, with a laundress next door to that! That was the pudding! In half a minute Mrs. Cratchit entered—flushed, but smiling proudly—with the pudding like a speckled cannon-ball, so hard and firm, blazing in half of half-a-quartern of ignited brandy, and bedight with Christmas holly stuck into the top.

Oh, a wonderful pudding! Bob Cratchit said, and calmly, too, that he regarded it as the greatest success achieved by Mrs. Cratchit since their marriage. Mrs. Cratchit said that, now the weight was off her mind, she would confess she had her doubts about the quantity of flour. Everybody had something to say about it, but nobody said or thought it was a small pudding for a large family. It would have been flat heresy to do so. Any Cratchit would have blushed to hint at such a thing.

At last the dinner was all done, the cloth was cleared, the hearth swept, and the fire made up. The compound in the jug being tasted, and considered perfect, apples and oranges were put upon the table, and a shovel full of chestnuts on the fire. Then all the Cratchit family drew round the hearth in what Bob Cratchit called a circle, meaning half a one; and at Bob Cratchit's elbow stood the family display of glass—two tumblers and a custard cup without a handle.

These held the hot stuff from the jug, however, as well as golden goblets would have done; and Bob served it out with beaming looks, while the chestnuts on the fire sputtered and cracked noisily. Then Bob proposed:

"A merry Christmas to us all, my dears. God bless us!"

Which all the family re-echoed.

"God bless us everyone!" said Tiny Tim, the last of all.

Now I told you that Mr. Scrooge had some disagreeable and wonderful dreams on Christmas eve, and so he
had; and in one of them he dreamt that a Christmas spirit
showed him his clerk's home; he saw them all gathered
round the fire, and heard them drink his health, and Tiny
Tim's song, and he took special note of Tiny Tim himself.

How Mr. Scrooge spent Christmas day we do not
know. He may have remained in bed, having a cold, but
on Christmas night he had more dreams. and the spirit took
him again to his clerk's poor home. The mother was doing
some needlework, seated by the table, a tear dropped on it
now and then, and she said, poor thing, that the work, which
was black, hurt her eyes. The children sat, sad and silent,
about the room, except Tiny Tim, who was not there. Upstairs the father, with his face hidden in his hands, sat
beside a little bed, on which lay a tiny figure, white and still.
"My little child, my pretty little child," he sobbed, as the
tears fell through his fingers on to the floor. "Tiny Tim
died because his father was too poor to give him what was
necessary to make him well; *you* kept him poor;" said the
dream-spirit to Mr. Scrooge. The father kissed the cold, little
face on the bed and went down stairs, where the sprays of
holly still remained about the humble room ; and taking his
hat, went out, with a wistful glance at the little crutch
in the corner as he shut the door. Mr. Scrooge saw all this,
and many more things as strange and sad—the spirit took
care of that; but, wonderful to relate, he woke the next morning feeling a different man—feeling as he had never felt in his
life before.

"Why, I am as light as a feather, and as happy as an
angel, and as merry as a schoolboy," he said to himself as he
absolutely skipped into the next room to breakfast and threw

on all the coal at once, and put two lumps of sugar in his tea. "I hope everybody had a merry Christmas, and here's a happy New Year to all the world."

Poor Bob Cratchit crept into the office a few minutes late, expecting to be roundly abused and scolded for it, but no

CRATCHIT AND MR. SCROOGE.

such thing; his master was there with his back to a good fire, and actually smiling, and he shook hands with his clerk, telling him heartily he was going to raise his salary, and asking quite affectionately after Tiny Tim! "And mind you make up a good fire in your room before you set to work, Bob," he said, as he closed his own door.

6

Bob could hardly believe his eyes and ears, but it was all true. Such doings as they had on New Year's day had never been seen before in the Cratchits' home, nor such a turkey as Mr. Scrooge sent them for dinner. Tiny Tim had his share, too, for Tiny Tim did not die, not a bit of it. Mr. Scrooge was a second father to him from that day; he wanted for nothing, and grew up strong and hearty. Mr. Scrooge loved him, and well he might, for was it not Tiny Tim who had unconsciously, through the Christmas dream-spirit, touched his hard heart and caused him to become a good and happy man?

Christmas Carol

Little Dombey.

LITTLE DOMBEY was the son of a rich city merchant. Ever since his marriage, ten years before our story commences, Mr. Dombey had ardently desired to have a son. He was a cold, stern, and pompous man, whose life and interests were entirely absorbed in his business, which appeared to him to be the most important thing in the whole world. It was not so much that he wanted a son to love, and to love him, but because he was so desirous of having one to associate with himself in the business, and make the house once more Dombey & Son in fact, as it was in name, that the little boy who was at last born to him was so precious, and so eagerly welcomed.

There was a pretty little girl six years old, but her father had taken so little notice of her that it was doubtful if he would have known her had he met her in the street. Of what

use was a girl to Dombey & Son?　She could not go into
the business.

LITTLE DOMBEY AND HIS SISTER.
"He would laugh and hold out his arms as soon as she came in sight."

Little Dombey's mother died when he was born, but the
event did not greatly disturb Mr. Dombey; and since his son
lived, what did it matter to him that his little daughter

Florence was breaking her heart in loneliness for the mother who had loved and cherished her!

During the first few months of his life, little Dombey

DOMBEY AND SON.

grew and flourished; and as soon as he was old enough to take notice, there was no one he loved so well as his sister Florence. He would laugh and hold out his arms as soon as she came in sight, and the affection of her baby brother comforted the lonely little girl, who was never weary of waiting on and playing with him.

In due time the baby was taken to church, and baptized by the name of Paul (his father's name). A grand and stately christening it was, followed by a grand and stately feast; and little Paul, when he was brought in to be admired by the company, was declared by his godmother to be "an angel, and the perfect picture of his own papa."

Whether baby Paul caught cold on his christening day or not, no one could tell, but from that time he seemed to waste and pine; his healthy and thriving babyhood had received a check, and as for illnesses, "there never was a blessed dear so put upon," his nurse said. Every tooth cost him a fit, and as for chicken-pox, whooping-cough, and measles, they followed one upon the other, and, to quote Nurse Richards again, "seized and worried him like tiger cats," so that by the time he was five years old, though he had the prettiest, sweetest little face in the world, there was always a patient. wistful look upon it, and he was thin and tiny and delicate. He would be as merry and full of spirits as other children when playing with Florence in their nursery, but he soon got tired, and had such old-fashioned ways of speaking and doing th.ngs, that Richards often shook her head sadly over him.

When he sat in his little arm-chair with his father, after dinner, as Mr. Dombey would have him do every day, they were a strange pair—so like, and so unlike each other.

"What is money, papa?" asked Paul on one of these occasions, crossing his tiny arms as well as he could—just as his father's were crossed.

"Why, gold, silver, and copper; you know what it is well enough, Paul," answered his father.

"Oh, yes; I mean, what can money do?"

"Anything, everything—almost," replied Mr. Dombey, taking one of his son's wee hands, and beating it softly against his own.

Paul drew his hand gently away. "It didn't save me my mamma, and it can't make me strong and big," said he.

"Why you *are* strong and big, as big as such little people usually are," returned Mr. Dombey.

"No," replied Paul, sighing; "when Florence was as little as me, she was strong and tall, and did not get tired of playing as I do. I am *so* tired sometimes, papa."

Mr. Dombey's anxiety was aroused, and he summoned his sister, Mrs. Chick, to consult with him over Paul, and the doctor was sent for to examine him.

"The child is hardly so stout as we could wish," said the doctor; "his mind is too big for his body, he thinks too much —let him try sea-air—sea-air does wonders for children."

So it was arranged that Florence, Paul, and nurse should go to Brighton, and stay in the house of a lady named Mrs. Pipchin, who kept a very select boarding-house for children, and whose management of them was said, in the best circles, to be truly marvelous. Mr. Dombey himself went down to Brighton every week, and had the children to stay with him at his hotel from Saturday to Monday, that he might judge of the progress made by his son and heir towards health.

There is no doubt that, apart from his importance to the house of Dombey & Son, little Paul had crept into his father's heart, cold though it still was towards his daughter, colder than ever now, for there was in it a sort of unacknowledged jealousy of the warm love lavished on her by Paul, which he himself was unable to win.

LITTLE PAUL AND FLORENCE.

Mrs. Pipchin was a marvelously ugly old lady, with a hook nose and stern cold eyes. Two other children lived at present under her charge, a mild, blue-eyed little girl who was known as Miss Pankey, and a Master Bitherstone, a solemn and sad-looking little boy whose parents were in India, and who asked Florence in a depressed voice whether she could give him any idea of the way back to Bengal.

"Well, Master Paul, how do you think you will like me?" said Mrs. Pipchin, seeing the child intently regarding her.

"I don't think I shall like you at all," replied Paul, shaking his head. "I want to go away. I do not like your house."

Paul did not like Mrs. Pipchin, but he would sit in his arm-chair and look at her, just as he had looked at his father at home. Her ugliness seemed to fascinate him.

As the weeks went by little Paul grew more healthy-looking, but he did not seem to grow any stronger, and could not run about out of doors. A little carriage was therefore got for him, in which he could be wheeled down to the beach, where he would pass the greater part of the day.

Consistent in his odd tastes, the child set aside a ruddy-faced lad who was proposed as the drawer of his carriage, and selected, instead, his grandfather—a weazen, cold, crab-faced man, in a suit of battered oilskin, who had got tough and stringy from long pickling in salt water, and who smelt like a weedy seabeach when the tide is out.

With this notable attendant to pull him along, and Florence always walking by his side, and the despondent Wickam bringing up the rear, he went down to the margin of the ocean every day; and there he would sit or lie in his carriage for hours together; never so distressed as by the company of children—Florence alone excepted, always.

"Go away, if you please," he would say to any child who came to bear him company. "Thank you, but I don't want you."

Some small voice, near his ear, would ask him how he was, perhaps.

"I am very well, I thank you," he would answer. "But you had better go and play, if you please."

Then he would turn his head and watch the child away, and say to Florence, "We don't want any others, do we? Kiss me, Floy."

"I love you, Floy," he said one day to her; "if you went to India as that boy's sister did, I should die."

Florence laid her head against his pillow, and whispered how much stronger he was growing.

"Oh yes, I know, I am a great deal better," said Paul, "a very great deal better.   Listen, Floy; what is it the sea keeps saying?"

"Nothing, dear; it is only the rolling of the waves you hear."

"Yes, but they are always saying something, and always the same thing.   What place is over there, Floy?"

She told him there was another country opposite, but Paul said he did not mean that, he meant somewhere much farther away, oh, much farther away—and often he would break off in the midst of their talk to listen to the sea and gaze out toward that country "farther away."

After having lived at Brighton for a year, Paul was certainly much stronger, though still thin and delicate.   And on one of his weekly visits, Mr. Dombey observed to Mrs. Pipchin,with pompous condescension,"My son is getting on, Madam, he is really getting on.   He is six years of age, and six will be sixteen before we have time to look about us."

And then he went on to explain that Paul's weak health having kept him back in his studies, which, considering the great destiny before the heir of Dombey & Son, was much to be regretted, he had made arrangements to place him at the educational establishment of Dr. Blimber, which was close by. Florence was, for the present, to remain under Mrs. Pipchin's care, and see her brother every week.

Dr. Blimber's school was a great hot-house for the forcing of boys' brains; no matter how backward a boy was, Doctor Blimber could always bring him on, and make a man of him in no time; and Dr. Blimber promised speedily to make a man of Paul.

"Shall you like to be made a man of, my son?" asked Mr. Dombey.

"I'd rather be a child and stay with Floy," answered Paul.

Then a different life began for little Dombey.

Miss Blimber, the doctor's daughter, a learned lady in spectacles, was his special tutor, and from morning till night his poor little brains were forced and crammed, till his head was heavy and always had a dull ache in it, and his small legs grew weak again—every day he looked a little thinner and a little paler, and became more old-fashioned than ever in his looks and ways—"old-fashioned" was a distinguishing title which clung to him. He was gentle and polite to everyone —always looking out for small kindnesses which he might do to any inmate of the house. Everyone liked "little Dombey," but everyone down to the footman said with the same kind of a tender smile—he was such an old-fashioned boy. "The oddest and most old-fashioned child in the world," Dr. Blimber would say to his daugher; "but bring him on, Cornelia—bring him on."

And Cornelia did bring him on; and Florence, seeing how pale and weary the little fellow looked when he came to her on Saturdays, and how he could not rest for anxiety about his lessons, would lighten his labors a little, and ease his mind by helping him to prepare his week's work.

One of Paul's friends at Dr. Blimber's school was a Mr. Toots, a young gentleman with a swollen nose and an

FLORENCE AND LITTLE PAUL.

excessively large head. The people said that the doctor overdid it with young Toots, and that when he began to have whiskers he left off having brains.

One day, when his lessons were over, about a fortnight before the commencement of holidays, little Paul's head, which had long been ailing more or less, and was sometimes very heavy and painful, felt so uneasy that night that he was obliged to support it on his hand. And yet it drooped so, that by little and little it sank on Mr. Toots' knee, and rested there, as if it had no care ever to be lifted up again.

That was no reason why he should be deaf; but he must have been, he thought, for, by-and-by, he heard Mr. Feeder calling in his ear, and gently shaking him to rouse his attention. And when he raised his head, quite scared, and looked about him, he found that Doctor Blimber had come into the room, and that the window was open, and that his forehead was wet with sprinkled water; though how all this had been done without his knowledge was very curious indeed.

"Ah! Come, come! That's well! How is my little friend now?" said Doctor Blimber, encouragingly.

"Oh, quite well, thank you, sir," said Paul.

But there seemed to be something the matter with the floor, for he couldn't stand upon it steadily; and with the walls too, for they were inclined to turn round and round, and could only be stopped by being looked at very hard indeed. Mr. Toots' head had the appearance of being at once bigger and farther off than was quite natural; and when he took Paul in his arms, to carry him upstairs, Paul observed with astonishment that the door was in quite a different place from that in which he had expected to find it, and almost thought, at first, that Mr. Toots was going to walk straight up the chimney.

It was very kind of Mr. Toots, Paul's chief patron, to carry him to the top of the house so tenderly; and Paul told him that it was. But Mr. Toots said he would do a great deal more than that, if he could; and indeed he did more as it was, for he helped Paul to undress, and helped him to bed, in the kindest manner possible.

In a few days Paul was able to get up and creep about the house. He wondered sometimes why everyone looked at and spoke so very kindly to him, and was more than ever careful to do any little kindnesses he could think of for them; even the rough, ugly dog Diogenes, who lived in the yard, came in for a share of his attentions.

There was to be a party at Dr. Blimber's on the evening before the boys went home, and Paul wished to remain for this, because Florence was coming, and he wanted her to see how everyone was fond of him. He was to go away with her after the party. Paul sat in a corner of the sofa all the evening, and everyone was very kind to him, indeed, it was quite extraordinary, Paul thought, and he was very happy; he liked to see how pretty Florence was, and how everyone admired and wished to dance with her. When the time came for them to take leave, the whole houseful gathered on the steps to say good-by to little Dombey and his sister, Toots even opening the carriage-door to say it over again.

"Good-by, Dr. Blimber; said Paul, stretching out his hand.

"Good-by, my little friend," returned the doctor.

"I'm very much obliged to you, sir," said Paul, looking innocently up into his awful face. "Ask them to take care of Diogenes, if you please."

Diogenes was the dog, who had never in his life received a friend into his confidence before Paul. So the doctor promised that every attention should be paid to Diogenes in Paul's absence.

After resting for a night at Mrs. Pipchin's house, little Paul went home, and was carried straight upstairs to his bed.

"Floy, dear," said he to his sister, when he was comfortably settled, "was that papa in the hall when I was carried in?"

"Yes, dear," answered Florence.

"He didn't cry, did he, Floy, and go into his own room when he saw me?"

Florence could only shake her head and hide her face against his, as she kissed him.

"I should not like to think papa cried," murmured little Paul, as he went to sleep.

He lay in his bed day after day quite happily and patiently, content to watch and talk to Florence. He would tell her his dreams, and how he always saw the sunlit ripples of a river rolling, rolling fast in front of him; sometimes he seemed to be rocking in a little boat on the water and its motion lulled him to rest, and then he would be floating away, away to that shore farther off, which he could not see. One day he told Florence that the water was rippling brighter and faster than ever, and that he could not see anything else.

"My own boy, cannot you see your poor father?" said Mr. Dombey, bending over him.

"Oh yes; but don't be so sorry, dear papa, I am so happy—good-by, dear papa." Presently he opened his eyes again, and said, "Floy, mamma is like you, I can see her. Come close to me, Floy, and tell them," whispered the dying boy, "that the face of the picture of Christ on the staircase at school is not divine enough; the light from it is shining on me now, and the water is shining, too, and rippling so fast, so fast."

The evening light shone into the room, but little Paul's spirit had gone out on the rippling water, and the divine face was shining on him from the farther shore.

One day, about a week after the funeral, Florence was sitting at her work when Susan appeared, with a face half laughing and half crying, to announce a visitor.

"A visitor! To me, Susan?" said Florence, looking up in astonishment.

"Well, it *is* a wonder, ain't it now, Miss Floy," said Susan; "but I wish you had a many visitors, I do, indeed, for you'd be all the better for it, and it's my opinion that the sooner you and me goes even to them old Skettleses, Miss, the better for both. I may not wish to live in crowds, Miss Floy, but still I'm not an oyster."

To do Miss Nipper justice, she spoke more for her young mistress than herself; and her face showed it.

"But the visitor, Susan!" said Florence.

Susan, with an hysterical explosion that was as much a laugh as a sob, and as much a sob as a laugh, answered:

"Mr. Toots!"

The smile that appeared on Florence's face passed from it in a moment, and her eyes filled with tears. But at any rate it was a smile, and that gave great satisfaction to Miss Nipper.

"My own feelings exactly, Miss Floy," said Susan, putting her apron to her eyes, and shaking her head. "Immediately I see that innocent in the hall, Miss Floy, I burst out laughing first, and then I choked."

Susan Nipper involuntarily proceeded to do the like again on the spot. In the meantime Mr. Toots, who had come upstairs after her, all unconscious of the effect he produced, announced himself with his knuckles on the door, and walked in very briskly.

"How d'ye do, Miss Dombey," said Mr. Toots. "I am very well, I thank you; how are you?"

Mr. Toots—than whom there were few better fellows in the world, though there may have been one or two brighter spirits—had laboriously invented this long burst of discourse with the view of relieving the feelings both of Florence and himself. But finding that he had run through his property, as it were, in an injudicious manner, by squandering the whole before taking a chair, or before Florence had uttered a word, or before he had well got in at the door, he deemed it advisable to begin again.

MISS BLIMMER AND PAUL.

"How dy'e do, Miss Dombey?" said Mr. Toots. "I'm very well, I thank you; how are you?"

Florence gave him her hand, and said she was very well.

"I'm very well, indeed," said Mr. Toots, taking a chair. "Very well, indeed, I am. I don't remember," said Mr. Toots, after reflecting a little, "that I was ever better, thank you."

"It's very kind of you to come," said Florence, taking up her work. "I am very glad to see you."

Mr. Toots replied with a chuckle. Thinking that might be too lively, he corrected it with a sigh. Thinking that might be too melancholy, he corrected it with a chuckle.

7

Not thoroughly pleasing himself with either mode of reply, he breathed hard.

"You were very kind to my dear brother," said Florence, obeying her own natural impulse to relieve him by saying so. "He often talked to me about you."

"Oh, it's of no consequence," said Mr. Toots, hastily. "Warm, ain't it?"

"It's beautiful weather," replied Florence.

"It agrees with *me!*" said Mr. Toots. "I don't think I ever was so well as I find myself at present, I'm obliged to you."

After stating this curious and unexpected fact, Mr. Toots fell into a deep well of silence.

"You have left Dr. Blimber's, I think?" said Florence, t ing to help him out.

"I should hope so," returned Mr. Toots. And tumbled in again.

He remained at the bottom, apparently drowned, for at least ten minutes. At the expiration of that period he suddenly floated, and said:

"Well! Good-morning, Miss Dombey."

"Are you going?" asked Florence, rising.

"I don't know, though. No, not just at present," said Mr. Toots, sitting down again, most unexpectedly. "The fact is—I say, Miss Dombey!"

"Don't be afraid to speak to me," said Florence, with a quiet smile. "I should be very glad if you would talk about my brother."

"Would you, though," retorted Mr. Toots, with sympathy in every fibre of his otherwise expressionless face. "Poor Dombey! [I am sure I never thought that Burgess & Co.—fashionable tailors (but very dear), that we used to

talk about—would make this suit of clothes for such a purpose. Mr. Toots was dressed in mourning.] "Poor Dombey!
I say, Miss Dombey!" blubbered Toots.

"Yes," said Florence.

"There's a friend he took to very much at last. I
thought you'd like to have him, perhaps, as a sort of keepsake. You remember his remembering Diogenes?"

"Oh yes! oh yes!" cried Florence.

"Poor Dombey! So do I," said Mr. Toots.

Mr. Toots, seeing Florence in tears, had great difficulty
in getting beyond this point, and had nearly tumbled into
the well again. But a chuckle saved him on the brink.

"I say," he proceeded, "Miss Dombey! I could have
had him stolen for ten shillings, if they hadn't given him up,
and I would, but they were glad to get rid of him, I think.
If you'd like to have him, he's at the door. I brought him
on purpose for you. He ain't a lady's dog, you know,"
said Mr. Toots, "but you won't mind that, will you?"

In fact, Diogenes was at that moment, as they presently
ascertained from looking down into the street, staring through
the window of a hackney cabriolet, into which, for convey-
ance to that spot, he had been ensnared on a false pretense
of rats among the straw. Sooth to say, he was as unlike a
lady's dog as dog might be; and in his gruff anxiety to get
out presented an appearance sufficiently unpromising as he
gave short yelps out of one side of his mouth, and over-
balancing himself by the intensity of every one of those
efforts tumbled down into the straw, and then sprang, pant-
ing, up again, putting out his tongue, as if he had come
express to a dispensary to be examined for his health.

But though Diogenes was as ridiculous a dog as one
would meet with on a summer's day—a blundering, ill-

favored, clumsy, bullet-headed dog, continually acting on a wrong idea that there was an enemy in the neighborhood, whom it was meritorious to bark at; and though he was far from good-tempered, and certainly was not clever, and had hair

"I DON'T THINK I SHALL LIKE YOU AT ALL," REPLIED PAUL.

all over his eyes, and a comic nose, and an inconsistent tail and a gruff voice—he was dearer to Florence, in virtue of that parting remembrance of him and that request that he might be taken care of, than the most valuable and beauti-

ful of his kind. So dear, indeed, was this same ugly
Diogenes, and so welcome to her, that she took the jeweled
hand of Mr. Toots and kissed it in her gratitude. And when
Diogenes, released, came tearing up the stairs and, bouncing
into the room, dived under all the furniture, and wound a
long iron chain that dangled from his neck round legs of
chairs and tables, and then tugged at it until his eyes became
unnaturally visible, in consequence of their nearly starting
out of his head, and when he growled at Mr. Toots, who
affected familiarity, Florence was as pleased with him as if
he had been a miracle of discretion.

Mr. Toots was so overjoyed by the success of his
present, and was so delighted to see Florence bending down
over Diogenes, smoothing his coarse back with her delicate
little hand—Diogenes graciously allowing it from the first
moment of their acquaintance—that he felt it difficult to take
leave, and would, no doubt, have been a much longer time
in making up his mind to do so if he had not been assisted
by Diogenes himself, who suddenly took it into his head to
bay Mr. Toots, and to make short runs at him with his
mouth open. Not exactly seeing his way to the end of these
demonstrations, and sensible that they placed the pantaloons
constructed by the art of Burgess & Co. in jeopardy, Mr.
Toots, with chuckles, finally took himself off and got away.

"Come, then, Di! Dear Di! Make friends with your
new mistress. Let us love each other, Di!" said Florence,
fondling his shaggy head. And Di, the rough and gruff, as
if his hairy hide were pervious to the tear that dropped upon
it, and his dog's heart melted as it fell, put his nose up to her
face, and swore fidelity.

Diogenes the man did not speak plainer to Alexander
the Great than Diogenes the dog spoke to Florence. He

subscribed to the offer of his little mistress cheerfully, and devoted himself to her service. A banquet was immediately provided for him in a corner; and when he had eaten and drunk his fill he went to the window, where Florence was sitting, looking on, rose up on his hind legs, with his awkward forepaws on her shoulders, licked her face and hands, nestled his great head against her heart, and wagged his tail till he was tired. Finally, Diogenes coiled himself up at her feet and went to sleep.

The Runaway Couple.

"SUPPOSING a young gentleman not eight years old was to run away with a fine young woman of seven, would you consider that a queer start? That there is a start as I—the Boots at Holly-Tree Inn—have seen with my own eyes; and I cleaned the shoes they ran away in, and they was so little that I couldn't get my hand into 'em.

"Master Harry Walmers' father, he lived at the Elms, away by Shooter's Hill, six or seven miles from London. He was uncommon proud of Master Harry, as he was his only child; but he didn't spoil him, neither. He was a gentleman that had a will of his own, and an eye of his own, and that would be minded. Consequently, though he made quite a companion of the fine bright boy, still he kept the command over him, and the child *was* a child. I was under-gardener there at that time; and one morning Master Harry, he comes to me and says—

"'Cobbs, how should you spell Norah if you was asked?' and then began cutting it in print all over the fence.

"He couldn't say he had taken particular notice of children before that; but really it was pretty to see them two mites a-going about the place together, deep in love! And the courage of the boy! Bless your soul, he'd have throwed off his little hat, and tucked up his little sleeves, and gone in at a lion, he would, if they had happened to meet one and she had been frightened of him. One day he stops along with her, where Boots was hoeing weeds in the gravel, and says—speaking up, 'Cobbs,' he says, 'I like you.' 'Do you, sir? I'm proud to hear it.' 'Yes, I do, Cobbs. Why do I like you, do you think, Cobbs?' 'Don't know, Master

MASTER HARRY AND NORAH ARRIVE AT THE HOLLY-TREE INN.,

Harry, I am sure.' 'Because Norah likes you, Cobbs.'
'Indeed, sir? That's very gratifying.' 'Gratifying, Cobbs?
It's better than millions of the brightest diamonds to be
liked by Norah.' 'Certainly, sir.' 'You're going away,
ain't you, Cobbs?' 'Yes, sir.' 'Would you like another
situation, Cobbs?' 'Well, sir, I shouldn't object, if it was
a good 'un.' 'Then, Cobbs,' says he, 'you shall be our head
gardener when we are married.' And he tucks her, in her
little sky-blue mantle, under his arm, and walks away.

"It was better than a picter, and equal to a play, to see
them babies with their long, bright, curling hair, their sparkling eyes, and their beautiful light tread, a-rambling about
the garden, deep in love. Boots was of opinion that the
birds believed they was birds, and kept up with 'em, singing
to please 'em. Sometimes they would creep under the
Tulip tree, and would sit there with their arms round one
another's necks, and their soft cheeks touching, a-reading
about the prince and the dragon, and the good and bad en-
chanters, and the king's fair daughter. Sometimes he would
hear them planning about having a house in a forest, keeping bees and a cow, and living entirely on milk and honey.
Once he came upon them by the pond, and heard Master
Harry say: 'Adorable Norah, kiss me, and say you love me
to distraction, or I'll jump in headforemost.' And Boots
made no question he would have done it if she hadn't com-
plied.

"'Cobbs,' says Master Harry one evening when
Cobbs was watering the flowers, 'I am going on a visit, this
present mid-summer, to my grandmamma's at York.'

"'Are you, indeed, sir? I hope you'll have a pleasant
time. I am going into Yorkshire myself when I leave here.'

"'Are you going to your grandmamma's, Cobbs?'

"'No, sir. I haven't got such a thing.'

"'Not as a grand-mamma, Cobbs?'

"'No, sir.'

"The boy looked on at the watering of the flowers for a little while and then said, 'I shall be very glad, indeed, to go, Cobbs—Norah's going.'

"'You'll be all right then, sir,' says Cobbs, 'with your beautiful sweetheart by your side.'

'Cobbs,' returned the boy, flushing, 'I never let anybody joke about it when I can prevent them.'

"'It wasn't a joke, sir,' says Cobbs, with humility — 'wasn't so meant.'

"'I am glad of that, Cobbs, because I like you, you know, and you're going to live with us, Cobbs.'

"'Sir?'

MASTER HARRY AND NORAH.
"Walks into the house much bolder than brass."

"'What do you think my grandmamma gives me when I go down there?'

"'I couldn't so much as make a guess, sir.'

"'A Bank of England five-pound note, Cobbs.'

"'Whew!' says Cobbs, 'that's a spanking sum of money, Master Harry.'

"'A person could do a great deal with such a sum of money as that. Couldn't a person, Cobbs?'

"'I believe you, sir!'

"'Cobbs,' said the boy, 'I'll tell you a secret. At Norah's house they have been joking her about me, and pretending to laugh at our being engaged. Pretending to make game of it, Cobbs!'

"'Such, sir,' says Cobbs, 'is the depravity of human natur'.'

"The boy, looking exactly like his father, stood for a few minutes with his glowing face towards the sunset, and then departed with, 'Good-night, Cobbs. I'm going in.'

"I was the Boots at the Holly-Tree Inn when one summer afternoon the coach drives up, and out of the coach gets these two children.

"The guard says to our governor, 'I don't quite make out these little passengers, but the young gentleman's words was that they were to be brought here.' The young gentleman gets out, hands his lady out, gives the guard something for himself, says to our governor, 'We're to stop here to-night, please. Sitting room and two bedrooms will be required. Chops and cherry-pudding for two!' and tucks her, in her little sky-blue mantle, under his arm and walks into the house much bolder than brass.

"Boots leaves me to judge what the amazement of that establishment was when those two tiny creatures, all alone by themselves, was marched into the Angel—much more so when he, who had seen them without their seeing him, give the governor his views of the expedition they was upon. 'Cobbs,' says the governor, 'if this is so, I must set off myself to York and quiet their friends' minds. In which case you must keep your eye upon 'em, and humor 'em, till I come back. But before I take these measures, Cobbs, I should wish you to find out from themselves whether your

"**And** they laid down on a bank of daisies and fell asleep."

opinions is correct.' 'Sir to you,' says Cobbs, 'that shall be done directly.'

"So Boots goes up stairs to the Angel, and there he finds Master Harry on an enormous sofa a-drying the eyes of Miss Norah with his pocket-hankercher. Their little legs were entirely off the ground of course, and it really is not possible for Boots to express to me how small them children looked.

"It's Cobbs! It's Cobbs!' cries Master Harry, and comes running to him, and catching hold of his hand. Miss Norah comes running to him on t'other side, and catching hold of his t'other hand, and they both jump for joy.

"'I see you a-getting out, sir,' says Cobbs. 'I thought it was you. I thought I couldn't be mistaken in your height and figure. What's the object of your journey, sir?—matrimonial?'"

"'We are going to be married, Cobbs, at Gretna Green,' returned the boy. 'We have run away on purpose. Norah has been in rather low spirits, Cobbs; but she'll be happy, now we have found you to be our friend.'

"'Thank you, sir, and thank *you*, miss,' says Cobbs, 'for your good opinion. *Did* you bring any luggage with you, sir?'

"If I will believe Boots when he gives me his word and honor upon it, the lady had got a parasol, a smelling-bottle, a round and a half of cold buttered toast, eight peppermint drops, and a hair-brush—seemingly a doll's. The gentleman had got about half a dozen yards of string, a knife, three or four sheets of writing-paper folded up surprisingly small, an orange, and a Chaney mug with his name upon it.

"'What may be the exact natur' of your plans, sir?' says Cobbs.

"'To go on,' replied the boy—which the courage of that boy was something wonderful!—'in the morning, and be married to-morrow.'

"'Just so, sir,' says Cobbs. 'Would it meet your views, sir, if I was to accompany you?'

"When Cobbs said this they both jumped for joy again, and cried out, 'Oh, yes, yes, Cobbs! Yes!'

"'Well, sir,' says Cobbs. 'If you will excuse my hav-

ing the freedom to give an opinion, what I should recom-
mend would be this. I'm acquainted with a pony, sir,
which, put in a phæton that I could borrow, would take you
and Mrs. Harry Walmers, Jr. (myself driving, if you ap-
prove), to the end of your journey in a very short space of
time. I am not altogether sure, sir, that this pony will be
at liberty to-morrow, but even if you had to wait over to-
morrow for him it might be worth your while. As to the
small account here, sir, in case you was to find yourself running at all short, that don't signify, because I'm a part pro-
prietor of this inn, and it could stand over.'

"Boots assures me that when they clapped their hands
and jumped for joy again, and called him 'Good Cobbs!'
and 'Dear Cobbs!' and bent across him to kiss one another
in the delight of their confiding hearts, he felt himself the
meanest rascal for deceiving 'em that ever was born.

"'Is there anything you want just at present, sir?' says
Cobbs, mortally ashamed of himself.

"'We would like some cakes after dinner,' answered
Master Harry, folding his arms, putting out one leg, and
looking straight at him, 'and two apples—and jam. With
dinner, we should like to have toast and water. But Norah
has always been accustomed to half a glass of currant wine
at dessert. And so have I.'

"'It shall be ordered at the bar, sir,' says Cobbs; and
away he went.

"The way in which the women of that house—without
exception—every one of 'em—married and single—took to
that boy when they heard the story, Boots considers surprising. It was as much as he could do to keep 'em from
dashing into the room and kissing him. They climbed up
all sorts of places, at the risk of their lives, to look at him

through a pane of glass. They were seven deep at the key-hole. They were out of their minds about him and his bold spirit.

"In the evening Boots went into the room, to see how the runaway couple was getting on. The gentleman was on the window-seat, supporting the lady in his arms. She had tears upon her face, and was lying, very tired and half-asleep, with her head upon his shoulder.

"'Mrs. Harry Walmers, Jr., fatigued, sir?' says Cobbs.

"'Yes, she is tired, Cobbs; but she is not used to be away from home, and she has been in low spirits again. Cobbs, do you think you could bring a biffin, please?'

"'I ask your pardon, sir,' says Cobbs. 'What was it you——'

"'I think a Norfolk biffin would rouse her, Cobbs. She is very fond of them.'

"Boots withdrew in search of the required restorative, and, when he brought it in, the gentleman handed it to the lady, and fed her with a spoon, and took a little himself. The lady being heavy with sleep, and rather cross, 'What should you think, sir,' says Cobbs, 'of a chamber candle-stick?' The gentleman approved; the chambermaid went first, up the great staircase; the lady, in her sky-blue mantle, followed, gallantly escorted by the gentleman; the gentleman embraced her at the door, and retired to his own apartment, where Boots softly locked him up.

"Boots couldn't but feel what a base deceiver he was when they asked him at breakfast (they had ordered sweet milk-and-water, and toast and currant jelly, overnight) about the pony. It really was as much as he could do, he don't mind confessing to me, to look them two young things in the face, and think how wicked he had grown up to be.

Howsomever, he went on a-lying like a Trojan, about the
pony. He told 'em it did so unfortunately happen that the
pony was half clipped, you see, and that he couldn't be
taken out in that state for fear that it should strike to his

"The lady followed, gallantly escorted by the gentleman."

inside, but that he'd be finished clipping in the course of
the day, and that to-morrow morning at eight o'clock the
phaeton would be ready. Boots' view of the whole case,
looking back upon it in my room, is, that Mrs. Harry
Walmers, Jr., was beginning to give in. She hadn't had
her hair curled when she went to bed, and she didn't seem

quite up to brushing it herself, and it's getting in her eyes put her out. But nothing put out Master Harry. He sat behind his breakfast cup, a-tearing away at the jelly, as if he had been his own father.

"After breakfast Boots is inclined to consider that they drawed soldiers—at least, he knows that many such was found in the fireplace, all on horseback. In the course of the morning Master Harry rang the bell—it was surprising how that there boy did carry on—and said in a sprightly way, 'Cobbs, is there any good walks in this neighborhood?'

"'Yes, sir,' says Cobbs. 'There's Love Lane.'

"'Get out with you, Cobbs!'—that was that there boy's expression—'you're joking.'

"'Begging your pardon, sir,' says Cobbs, 'there really is Love Lane. And a pleasant walk it is, and proud I shall be to show it to yourself and Mrs. Harry Walmers, Jr.'

"'Norah, dear,' said Master Harry, 'this is curious. We really ought to see Love Lane. Put on your bonnet, my sweetest darling, and we will go there with Cobbs.'

"Boots leaves me to judge what a beast he felt himself to be, when that young pair told him, as they all three jogged along together, that they had made up their minds to give him two thousand guineas a year as head-gardener, on account of his being so true a friend to 'em. Boots could have wished at the moment that the earth would have opened and swallowed him up; he felt so mean with their beaming eyes a-looking at him, and believing him. Well, sir, he turned the conversation as well as he could, and he took 'em down Love Lane to the water meadows, and there Master Harry would have drowned himself in half a moment more, a-getting out a water-lily for her—but nothing daunted that boy. Well, sir, they was tired out. All being so new and strange to 'em, they was tired as tired could be. And they laid down on a bank of daisies, like the children in the wood, leastways meadows, and fell asleep.

"Well, sir, they woke up at last, and then one thing was getting pretty clear to Boots, namely, that Mrs. Harry Walmers, Jr.'s temper was on the move. When Master Harry took her round the waist she said he 'teased her so,' and when he says, 'Norah, my young May Moon, your Harry tease you?' she tells him, 'Yes; and I want to go home!'

"However, Master Harry he kept up, and his noble heart was as fond as ever. Mrs. Walmers turned very sleepy about dusk and began to cry. Therefore, Mrs. Walmers went off to bed as per yesterday; and Master Harry ditto repeated.

"About eleven or twelve at night comes back the governor in a chaise, along with Mr. Walmers and an elderly lady. Mr. Walmers looks amused and very serious, both at once, and says to our missis, 'We are very much indebted to you, ma'am, for your kind care of our little children, which we can never sufficiently acknowledge. Pray, ma'am, where is my boy?' Our missis says, 'Cobbs has the dear children in charge, sir. Cobbs, show forty! Then he says to Cobbs, 'Ah, Cobbs! I am glad to see *you*. I understood you was here.' And Cobbs says, 'Yes, sir, your most obedient, sir.'

"I may be surprised to hear Boots say it, perhaps, but Boots assures me that his heart beat like a hammer, going upstairs. 'I beg your pardon, sir,' says he, while unlocking the door; 'I hope you are not angry with Master Harry. For Master Harry is a fine boy, sir, and will do you credit and honor.' And Boots signifies to me that if the fine boy's father had contradicted him in the daring state of mind in which he then was, he thinks he should have 'fetched him a crack,' and taken the consequences.

"But Mr. Walmers only says, 'No, Cobbs. No, my good fellow. Thank you.' And the door being open, goes in.

"Boots goes in, too, holding the light, and he sees Mr. Walmers go up to the bedside, bend gently down, and kiss the little sleeping face. Then he stands looking at it for a minute, looking wonderfully like it; and then he gently shakes the little shoulder.

"'Harry, my dear boy! Harry!'

"Master Harry starts up and looks at him. Looks at Cobbs, too. Such is the honor of that mite that he looks at Cobbs to see whether he has brought him into trouble.

"'I am not angry, my child. I only want you to dress yourself and come home.'

"'Yes, Pa.'

"Master Harry dresses himself quickly. His breast begins to swell when he has nearly finished, and it swells more and more as he stands a-looking at his father; his father standing a-looking at him, the quiet image of him.

"'Please may I'—the spirit of that little creatur', and the way he kept his rising tears down—'Please, dear Pa—may I—kiss Norah before I go?'

"'You may, my child.'

"So he takes Master Harry in his hand, and Boots leads the way with the candle, and they come to that other bedroom, where the elderly lady is seated by the bed, and poor little Mrs. Harry Walmers, Jr., is fast asleep. There the father lifts the child up to the pillow, and he lays his little face down for an instant by the little warm face of poor un-

conscious little Mrs. Harry Walmers, Jr., and gently draws
it to him—a sight so touching to the chambermaids who are
peeping through the door that one of them calls out, 'It's a
shame to part 'em!'   But this chambermaid was always, as
Boots informs me, a soft-hearted one.   Not that there was
any harm in that girl.   Far from it."

Poor Jo!

JO AND THE BEADLE.

JO was a crossing-sweeper; his crossing was in Holborn, and there every day he swept up the mud, and begged for pennies from the people who passed. Poor Jo wasn't at all pleasant to look at. He wasn't pretty and he wasn't clean. His clothes were only a few poor rags that hardly protected him from the cold and the rain. He had never been to school, and he could neither write nor read—could not even spell his own name. He had only one name, Jo, and that served him for Christian and surname too.

Poor Jo! He was ugly, dirty and ignorant; but he knew one thing, that it was wicked to tell a lie, and knowing this, he always told the truth. One other thing poor Jo knew too well, and that was what being hungry means. For little Jo was very poor. He lived in Tom-all-Alones, one of the most horrible places in all London. The road here is thick with mud. The crazy houses are dropping away; two of them, Jo remembered, once fell to pieces. The air one breathes here is full of fever. The people who live in this dreadful den are the poorest of London poor. All miserably clad, all dirty, all

very hungry. They know and like Jo, for he is always willing to go on errands for them, and does them many little acts
of kindness. Not that they speak of him as Jo.

Oh, dear no! No one in Tom-all-Alones is spoken of
by his name, whether it be his surname, or that which his
godfathers and godmothers—always supposing that he had
any—gave him. The ladies and gentlemen who live in this
unfashionable neighborhood have their fashions just as much
as the great folks who live in the grand mansions in the West
End. Here one of the prevailing customs is to give everyone a
nickname. Thus it is that if you inquired there for a boy
named Jo you would be asked whether you meant Carrots, or
the Colonel, or Gallows, or young Chisel, or Terrier Tip, or
or Lankey, the Brick.

Jo was generally called Toughy, although a few superior persons who gave themselves airs and graces, and
affected a dignified style of speaking, called him "the tough
subject."

Jo used to say he had never had but one friend.

It was one cold winter night, when he was shivering in a
doorway near his crossing, that a dark-haired, rough-bearded
man turned to look at him, and then came back and began to
talk to him.

"Have you a friend, boy?" he asked presently.

"No, never 'ad none."

"Neither have I. Not one. Take this, and good-night,"
and so saying the man, who looked very poor and shabby,
put into Jo's hand the price of a supper and a night's lodging.

Often afterwards the stranger would stop to talk with
Jo, and give him money, Jo firmly believed, whenever he
had any to give. When he had none he would merely say,
"I am as poor as you are to-day, Jo," and pass on.

One day Jo was fetched away from his crossing by the
Beadle, and taken by him to the Sol's Arms, a public house
in a little court near Chancery Lane, where the Coroner was
holding an inquest—an "inkwich" Jo called it.

"Did the boy know the deceased?" asked the Coroner.

Indeed Jo had known him; it was his only friend who
was dead.

"He was very good to me, he was," was all poor Jo
could say.

The next day they buried the dead man in the churchyard hard by ; a churchyard hemmed in by houses on either
side, and separated by an iron gate from the wretched court
through which one goes to it.

But that night there came a slouching figure through
the court to the iron gate. It held the gate with both hands
and looked between the bars—stood looking in for a little
while, then with an old broom it softly swept the step and
made the archway clean. It was poor Jo; and as, after one
more long look through the bars of the gate, he went away
he softly said to himself, "He was very good to me, he
was."

Now, there happened to be at the inquest a kind-hearted
little man named Snagsby, who was a stationer by trade,
and he pitied Jo so much that he gave him half a crown.
Half a crown was Mr. Snagsby's one remedy for all the
troubles of this world.

Jo was very sad after the death of his one friend. The
more so as his friend had died in great poverty and misery,
with no one near him to care whether he lived or not.

It was a few days after the funeral, while Jo was still
living on Mr. Snagsby's half crown—half a bill, Jo called
it—that a much bigger slice of good luck fell to his share.

He was standing at his crossing as the day closed in, when
a lady closely veiled and plainly dressed came up to him.

JO AND HIS FRIEND.

"Are you the boy Jo who was examined at the inquest?"
she asked.

"That's me," said Jo.

"Come farther up the court. I want to speak to you."

"Wot, about him as was dead? Did you know him?"

"How dare you ask me if I knew him!"

"No offense, my lady," said Jo humbly.

"Listen and hold your tongue. Show me the place where he lived, then where he died, then where they buried him. Go in front of me, don't look back once, and I'll pay you well."

"I'm fly," said Jo. "But no larks, yer know. Stow hooking it."

Jo takes her to each of the places she wants to see, and he notices that when he shows her the burying-place she shrinks into a dark corner as if to hide herself while she looks at the spot where the dead man's body rests. Then she draws off her glove, and Jo sees that she has sparkling rings on her fingers. She drops a coin into his hand and is gone. Jo holds the coin to the light and sees to his joy that it is a golden sovereign. He bites it to make sure that it

JO AT THE GATE OF THE CHURCHYARD
WHERE THEY BURIED HIS FRIEND.

is genuine, and being satisfied that it has successfully stood the test he puts it under his tongue for safety, and goes off to Tom-all-Alones.

But people in Jo's position in life find it hard to change a sovereign, for who will believe that they can come by it

honestly? So poor little Jo didn't get much of the sovereign
for himself, for, as he afterwards told Mr. Snagsby—

"I had to pay five bob down in Tom-all-Alones before
they'd square it for to give me change, and then a young
man he thieved another five while I was asleep, and a boy
he thieved ninepence, and the landlord he stood drains round
with a lot more of it."

And so Jo was left alone in the world again, now his
friend was dead. And this poor friend had only two
mourners, Jo, the crossing sweeper, and the lady who had
come to look at his grave.

Jo mourned for him because he had been his only friend,
and the lady mourned for the poor man because she had
loved him dearly many years ago when they had both been
young together.

As time went on Jo's troubles began in earnest. The
police turned him away from his crossing, and wheresoever
they met him they ordered him to "move on." It was hard,
very hard on poor Jo; for he knew no way of getting a living
except at his crossing. So he would go back to it as often as
he dared, until the police turned him away again. Once a
policeman, angry to find that Jo hadn't moved on, seized
him by the arm and dragged him down to Mr. Snagsby's.

"What's the matter, constable?" asked Mr. Snagsby.

"This boy's as obstinate a young gonoph as I know;
although repeatedly told to, he won't move on."

"I'm always a-moving on," cried Jo. "Oh, my eye,
where am I to move to?"

"My instructions don't go to that," the constable
answered; "my instructions are that you're to keep moving
on. Now the simple question is, sir," turning to Mr.
Snagsby, "whether you know him. He says you do."

"Yes, I know him."

"Very well, I leave him here ; but mind you keep moving on."

The constable then moved on himself, leaving Jo at Mr. Snagsby's. There was a little tea party there that evening, and one of the guests, a very greasy, oily-looking man, whom they called Mr. Chadband, and who was a dissenting minister, having by this time eaten and drunk a great deal more than was good for him, determined to improve the occasion by delivering a discourse on Jo. It was very long and very dull to Jo; all he could remember of the sermon was this couplet—

"Oh running stream of sparkling joy,
To be a soaring human boy."

What he remembered better was, when the perspiring Chadband had finished, and he was at last allowed to go, Mr. Snagsby followed him to the door and filled his hands with the remains of the little feast they had had up stairs.

And now Jo began to find life rougher and harder than ever He lost his crossing altogether, and spent day after day in moving on. He grew hungrier and thinner, and at last the foul air of Tom-all-Alones began to have an ill-effect even on him—"the tough subject." His throat grew very dry, his cheeks were burning hot, and his poor little head ached till the pain made him cry. Then he remembered a poor woman he had once done a kindness to, a brickmaker's wife, who had told him she lived at St. Albans, and that a lady there had been very good to her. "Perhaps she'll be good to me," thought Jo, and he started off to go to St. Albans.

So it came about that one Saturday night Jo reached that town very tired and very ill. Happily for him the brickmaker's wife met him and took him into her cottage. While he was resting there a lady came in.

The lady sat down by the bed, and asked him very kindly what was the matter.

"I'm a-being froze and then burnt up, and then froze and burnt up again ever so many times over in an hour. And my head's all sleepy, and all a-going round like, and I'm so dry, and my bones is nothing half so much bones as pain."

"Where are you going?"

"Somewheres," replied Jo; "I'm a-being moved on, I am."

"Well, to-night you must come with me, and I'll make you comfortable." So Jo went with the lady to a great house not far off, and there in a nice warm loft they made a bed for him, and brought him tempting wholesome food. every one was very kind to him, even the servants called him "Old Chap," and told him he would soon be well. Jo was really happy, and for a time forgot his pain and fever. But something frightened Jo, and he felt he could not stay there, and he ran out into the cold night-air. Where he went he could never remember, for when he next came to his senses he found himself in a hospital. He stayed there for some weeks and was then discharged, though still weak and ill. He was very thin, and when he drew a breath his chest was very painful. "It draws," said Jo, "as heavy as a cart." Now a certain young doctor by the name of Allan Woodcourt, rather than count the hours on a restless pillow, takes a stroll on Tom-all-Alones one morning. The banks of a stagnant channel of mud is the main street of Tom-all-Alones; nothing is to be seen but the crazy houses, shut up and silent. No waking creature save himself appears, exccpt in one direction, where he sees the solitary figure of a woman sitting on a doorstep. He walks that way. Approaching, he ob- serves that she has journeyed a long dis- tance, and is foot- sore and travel-stained. She sits on the doorstep in the manner of one who is wait- ing, with her elbow on her knee and her head upon her hand. Beside her is a canvas bag, or bundle, she has carried. She is doz- ing probably, for she gives no heed to his steps as he comes towards her.

The broken footway is so narrow that, when the doctor

POOR JO, THE CROSSING SWEEPER.

comes to where the woman sits, he has to turn into the road to pass her. Looking down at her face his eye meets hers, and he stops.

"What is the matter?"

"Nothing, sir."

"Can't you make them hear? Do you want to be let in?"

"I'm waiting till they get up at another house—a lodging house—not here," the woman patiently returns. "I'm waiting here because there will be sun here presently to warm me."

"I am afraid you are tired. I am sorry to see you sitting in the street."

"Thank you, sir. It don't matter."

"I suppose you have some settled home? Is it far from here?" he asks, good-humoredly making light of what he has done, as she gets up and courtesies.

"It's a good two or three-and-twenty mile from here, sir. At Saint Albans. Do you know St. Albans, sir? I thought you gave a start like as if you did."

"Yes, I know something of it. And now I will ask you a question in return. Have you money for your lodging?"

Yes, sir," she says, "really and truly." And she shows it. He tells her, in acknowledgment of her many subdued thanks, that she is very welcome, gives her good-day, and walks away. Tom-all-Alones is still asleep, and nothing is astir.

Yes, something is! As he retraces his way to the point from which he saw the woman at a distance sitting on the step he sees a ragged figure coming very carefully along, crouching close to the soiled walls—which the wretchedest figure might as well avoid—and thrusting a hand before it. It is the figure of a boy, whose face is hollow, and whose eyes have an emaciated glare. He is so intent on getting along unseen that even the appearance of a stranger in whole garments does not tempt him to look back. He shades his face with his ragged elbow as he passes on the other side of the way, and goes shrinking and creeping on, with his anxious hand before him, and his shapeless clothes hanging in shreds. Clothes made for what purpose, or of what material, it would be impossible to say. They look, in color and in substance, like a bundle of rank leaves of swampy growth that rotted long ago.

Allan Woodcourt pauses to look after him and note all this, with a shadowy belief that he has seen the boy before. He cannot recall how, or where; but there is some association in his mind with such a form. He imagines that he must have seen it in some hospital or refuge; still, cannot make out why it comes with any special force on his remembrance.

He is gradually emerging from Tom-all-Alones in the morning light, thinking about it, when he hears running feet behind him; and looking round sees the boy scouring towards him at great speed, followed by the woman.

"Stop him, stop him!" cries the woman almost breathless. "Stop him, sir!".

He darts across the road into the boy's path, but the boy is quicker than he—makes a curve—ducks—dives under his hands—comes up half-a-dozen yards beyond him, and scours away again. Still the woman follows, crying, "Stop him, sir; pray stop him!" Allan, not knowing but that he has just robbed her of her money, follows in chase, and runs so hard that he runs the boy down nearly a dozen times; but each time he repeats the curve, the duck, the dive, and scours away again. To strike at him, on any of these occasions, would be to fell and disable him; but the pursuer cannot resolve to do that; and so the grimly ridiculous pursuit continues.   At last the fugitive, hard-pressed, takes to a narrow passage and a court which has no thoroughfare.   Here, against a hoarding of decaying timber, he is brought to bay, and tumbles down, lying gasping at his pursuer, who stands and gasps at him until the woman comes up.

"O you Jo!" cries the woman.   "What? I have found you at last!"

"Jo," repeats Allan, looking at him with attention. "Jo! Stay. To be sure! I recollect this lad some time ago being brought before the Coroner."

"Yes, I see you once afore at the inkwich," whimpers Jo.   "What of that? Can't you never let such an unfortnet as me alone? Ain't I unfortnet enough for you yet? How unfortnet do you want me fur to be? I've been a-chivied and a-chivied, fust by one on you and nixt by another on you, till I'm worrited to skins and bones. The inkwich warn't *my* fault. *I* done nothink. He wos wery good to me, he wos; he wos the only one I knowed to speak to, as ever come across my crossing. It ain't wery likely I should want him to be inkwiched. I only wish I wos, myself. I don't know why I don t go and make a hole in the water, I'm sure I don't."

He says it with such a pitiable air, and his grimy tears appear so real, and he lies in the corner up against the hoarding so like a growth of fungus, or any unwholesome ex-crescence produced there in neglect and impurity, that Allan Woodcourt is softened towards him.   He says to the woman, "Miserable creature, what has he done?"

To which she only replies, shaking her head at the prostrate figure more amazedly than angrily: "O you Jo, you Jo. I have found you at last!"

"What has he done?" says Allan. "Has he robbed you?"

"No, sir, no. Robbed me? He did nothing but what was kind-hearted by me, and that's the wonder of it."

Allan looks from Jo to the woman, and from the woman to Jo, waiting for one of them to unravel the riddle.

"But he was along with me, sir," says the woman— "O you Jo!—he was along with me, sir, down at Saint Albans, ill, and a young lady, Lord bless her for a good friend to me, took pity on him when I durstn't, and took him home—"

Allan shrinks back from him with a sudden horror.

"Yes, sir, yes. Took him home, and made him comfortable, and like a thankless monster he ran away in the night, and never has been seen or heard of since, till I set eyes on him just now. And that young lady that was such a pretty dear caught his illness, lost her beautiful looks, and wouldn't hardly be known for the same young lady now, if it wasn't for her angel temper, and her pretty shape, and her sweet voice. Do you know it? You ungrateful wretch, do you know that this is all along of you and of her goodness to you?" demands the woman, beginning to rage at him as she recalls it, and breaking into passionate tears.

The boy, in rough sort stunned by what he hears, falls to smearing his dirty forehead with his dirty palm, and to staring at the ground, and to shaking from head to foot until the hoarding against which he leans rattles.

Allan restrains the woman, merely by a quiet gesture, but effectually.

"You hear what she says. But get up, get up!"

Jo, shaking and chattering, slowly rises, and stands, after the manner of his tribe in a difficulty, sideways against

9

the hoarding, resting one of his high shoulders against it, and covertly rubbing his right hand over his left, and his left foot over his right.

"You hear what she says, and I know it's true. Have you been here ever since?"

"Wishermaydie if I seen Tom-all-Alones till this blessed morning," replies Jo, hoarsely.

"Why have you come here now?"

Jo looks all around the confined court, looks at his questioner no higher than the knees, and finally answers:

"I don't know how to do nothink, and I can't get nothink to do. I'm wery poor and ill, and I thought I'd come back here when there warn't nobody about, and lay down and hide somewheres as I knows on till arter dark, and then go and beg a trifle of Mr. Snagsby. He was allus willin' for give me somethink, he wos, though Mrs. Snagsby she wos allus a-chivying on me—like everybody everywheres."

"Where have you come from?"

Jo looks all around the court again, looks at his questioner's knees again, and concludes by laying his profile against the hoarding in a sort of resignation.

"Did you hear me ask you where you have come from?"

"Tramp then," says Jo.

"Now, tell me," proceeds Allan, making a strong effort to overcome his repugnance, going very near to him, and leaning over him with an expression of confidence, "tell me how it came about that you left that house, when the good young lady had been so unfortunate as to pity you, and take you home."

Jo suddenly comes out of his resignation, and excitedly declares, addressing the woman, that he never known about the young lady, that he never heern about it, that he never

went fur to hurt her, that he would sooner have hurt his own
self, that he'd sooner have had his unfortnet 'ead chopped
off than ever gone a-nigh her, and that she wos very good to
him, she wos. Conducting himself throughout as if in his
poor fashion he really meant it and winding up with some
very miserable sobs.

Allan Woodcourt sees that this is not a sham. He
constrains himself to touch him. "Come, Jo. Tell me?"

"No. I dustn't" says Jo, relapsing into the profile
state. "I dustn't, or I would."

"But I must know," returns the other, "all the same.
Come, Jo."

After two or three such adjurations, Jo lifts up his head
again, looks round the court again, and says in a low voice,
"Well, I'll tell you somethink. I was took away. There!"

"Took away? In the night?"

"Ah!" Fearful of being overheard, Jo looks about
him, and even glances up some ten feet at the top of the
hoarding, and through the cracks in it, lest the object of his
distrust should be looking over, or hidden on the other side.

"Who took you away?"

"I dustn't name him," says Jo. "I dustn't do it, sir."

"But I want, in the young lady's name, to know. You
may trust me. No one else shall hear."

"Ah, but I don't know," replies Jo, shaking his head
fearfully, "as he *don't* hear."

"Why, he is not in this place."

"Oh, ain't he though?" says Jo. "He's in all manner
of places, all at wunst."

Allan looks at him in perplexity, but discovers some
real meaning and good faith at the bottom of this bewilder-
ing reply. He patiently awaits an answer; and Jo, more

baffled by his patience than by anything else, at last des-
perately whispers a name in his ear.

"Ay!" says Allan. "Why, what had you been doing?"

"Nothink, sir, Never done nothink to get myself into
no trouble, 'sept in not moving on and the inkwich. But
I'm a-moving on now. I'm a-moving on to the berryin
ground—that's the move as I'm up to."

"No, no, we will try to prevent that. But what did he
do with you?"

"Put me in a horsepittle," replied Jo, whispering, "till
I was discharged, then giv' me a little money—four half-
bulls, wot you may call half-crowns—and ses 'Hook it!
Nobody wants you here,' he ses. 'You hook it. You go
and tramp,' he ses. 'You move on,' he ses. 'Don't let me
ever see you nowheres within forty miles of London, or you'll
repent it.' So I shall, if ever he does 'see me, and he'll see
me if I'm above ground," concludes Jo, nervously repeating
all his former precautions and investigations.

Allan considers a little; then says, turning to the
woman, but keeping an encouraging eye on Jo: "He is not
so ungrateful as you supposed. He had a reason for going
away, though it was an insufficient one."

"Thank'ee, sir, thank'ee!" exclaims Jo. "There now!
See how hard you wos upon me. But only you tell the
young lady wot the genlmn ses, and it's all right. For *you*
wos very good to me, too, and I knows it."

"Now, Jo," says Allan, keeping his eye upon him,
"come with me, and I will find you a better place than this
to lie down and hide in. If I take one side of the way and
you the other, to avoid observation, you will not 'hook it,'
I know very well, if you make me a promise."

"I won't not unless I was to see *him* a-coming, sir."

"Very well. I take your word. Half the town is getting up by this time, and the whole town will be broad awake in another hour. Come along. Good-day again, my good woman."

So Jo was taken to a clean little room, and bathed, and had clean clothes, and good food, and kind people about him once more, but he was too ill now, far too ill, for any-thing to do him any good.

"Let me lie here quiet," said poor Jo, "and be so kind anyone as is passin' nigh where I used to sweep, as to say to Mr. Snagsby as Jo, wot he knew once, is a-moving on."

One day the young doctor was sitting by him, when suddenly Jo made a strong effort to get out of bed.

"Well, Jo" what is the matter? "Don't be frightened."

"I thought," says Jo, who has started and is looking round, "I thought I was in Tom-all-Alones again. An't there nobody here but you, Mr. Woodcourt?"

"Nobody."

"And I an't took back to Tom-all-Alones. Am I, sir?"

"No." Jo closes his eyes, muttering, "I'm wery thankful."

After watching him closely a little while, Allan puts his mouth very near his ear, and says to him in a low, distinct voice:

"Jo! Did you ever know a prayer?"

"Never know'd nothink, sir."

"Not so much as one short prayer?"

"No, sir. Nothink at all. Mr. Chadbands he wos a-prayin' wunst at Mr. Snagsby's and I heerd him, but he sounded as if he was a-speakin' to his-self, and not to me. He prayed a lot, but *I* couldn't make out nothink on it. Different times there wos other genlmen come down Tom-all-Alones a-prayin', but they all mostly sed as the t'other wuns prayed wrong, and all mostly sounded to be a-talking to their-selves, or a passing blame on the t'others, and not a-talkin' to us. *We* never know'd nothink. *I* never know'd what it wos all about."

It takes him a long time to say this; and few but an experienced and attentive listener could hear, or, hearing, un-derstand him. After a short relapse into sleep or stupor, he makes, of a sudden, a strong effort to get out of bed.

"Stay, Jo, stay! What now?"

"It's time for me to go to that there berryin' ground, sir," he returns with a wild look.

"Lie down, and tell me. What burying ground, Jo?"

"Where they laid him as wos wery good to me, wery good to me indeed, he wos. It's time for me to go down to that there berryin' ground, sir, and ask to be put along with him. I wants to go there and be berried. He used fur to say to me, 'I am as poor as you to-day, Jo,' he ses. I wants to tell him that I am as poor as him now, and have come there to be laid along with him."

"By-and-by, Jo. By-and-by."

"Ah! P'r'aps they wouldn't do it if I wos to go myself. But will you promise to have me took there, sir, and laid along with him?"

"I will, indeed."

"Thank'ee, sir. Thank'ee, sir! They'll have to get the key of the gate afore they can take me in, for it's allus locked. And there's a step there, as I used fur to clean with my broom. It's turned wery dark, sir. Is there any light a-comin'?"

"It is coming fast, Jo."

Fast. The cart is shaken all to pieces, and the rugged road is very near its end.

"Jo, my poor fellow!"

"I hear you, sir, in the dark, but I'm a-gropin'—a-gropin' —let me catch hold of your hand."

"Jo, can you say what I say?"

"I'll say anythink as you say, sir, for I knows it's good."

"OUR FATHER."

"Our Father!—yes, that's wery good, sir!"

"WHICH ART IN HEAVEN."

"Art in Heaven—is the light a-comin', sir?"

"It is close at hand.   HALLOWED BE THY NAME."

"Hallowed be—Thy—name!"

The light is come upon the dark, benighted way.   Dead!

Dead, your majesty.   Dead, my lords and gentlemen. Dead, Right Reverends and Wrong Reverends of every order.   Dead, men and women born with heavenly compassion in your hearts.   And dying thus around us every day!

The Little Kenwigs.

WHAT an odd-looking family! What are they all in such distress about?

This is Mrs. Kenwigs, and those funny little girls are her daughters; and we shall see presently what is the cause of their grief.

Mrs. Kenwigs was the wife of an ivory turner, and though they only had a very humble home of two rooms in a dingy-looking house in a small street, they had great pretensions to being "genteel," and Mrs. Kenwigs was the admiration of all the neighbors. The little Misses Kenwigs had their flaxen hair plaited into pig-tails and tied with blue ribbons, and wore little white trousers with frills round their ankles, the highest fashion of that day; besides being dressed with such elegance, the two eldest girls went twice a week to a dancing school. Mrs. Kenwigs, too, had an uncle who collected the water-rate, and she was therefore considered a person of great distinction, with quite the manners of a lady. Now, it happened that on the eighth anniversary of their wedding-day Mr. and Mrs. Kenwigs decided to invite a party of friends to supper to celebrate the occasion. The four

eldest children were to be allowed to sit up to supper, and
the uncle, Mr. Lillyvick, the collector, had promised to come.
The baby was put to bed in a little room lent by one of the
lady guests, and a little girl hired to watch him, and Mrs.
Kenwigs, in a beautiful new gown, received her visitors in
great state. All the company had assembled when a ring
was heard, and Morleena, whose name had been *invented by
Mrs. Kenwigs* especially for her, ran down to open the door
and lead in her distinguished great-uncle, then the supper
was brought in and the party commenced.

The supper consisted of a pair of boiled fowls, a large
piece of pork, potatoes and greens, and an apple-pie, which
they all enjoyed amazingly.

Everybody had eaten everything, the table was cleared,
Mr. Lillyvick established in the arm-chair by the fireside,
the four little girls arranged on a small form in front of
the company with their flaxen tails toward them, when
Mrs. Kenwigs was suddenly dissolved in tears and sobbed
out—

"They are so beautiful!"

"Oh dear," said all the ladies, "so they are; it's very
natural you should feel proud of that; but don't give way,
don't."

"I can—not help it, and it don't signify," sobbed Mrs.
Kenwigs; "oh! they're too beautiful to live, much too beautiful."

On hearing this dismal prophecy all four little girls
screamed until their light flaxen tails vibrated again, and
rushed to bury their heads in their mother's lap, and she
clasped them in her arms.

At length she was soothed and the children calmed
down; while the ladies and gentlemen all said they were

sure they would live for many, many years, and there was no occasion for their mother's distress; and as the children were not so remarkably lovely, this was quite true.

Then Mr. Lillyvick talked to the company about his niece's marriage, and said graciously that he had always found Mr. Kenwigs a very honest, well-behaved, upright, and respectable sort of man, and shook hands with him, and then Morleena and her sisters kissed their uncle and most of the guests.

Then Miss Petowker, who was the daughter of a theatrical fireman, who went on in the pantomime, and who could sing and recite in a way that brought tears to Mrs. Kenwigs' eyes, remarked—

"Oh, dear Mrs. Kenwigs, while Mr. Noggs is making that punch to drink happy returns in, do let Morleena go through that figure dance before Mr. Lillyvick."

"No, no, my dear," replied Mrs. Kenwigs, "it will only worry my uncle."

"It can't worry him, I'm sure," said Miss Petowker. "You will be very much pleased, won't you, sir?"

"That I am sure I shall," replied the collector, glancing at the punch mixer.

"Well, then, I'll tell you what," said Mrs. Kenwigs. "Morleena shall do the steps if uncle can persuade Miss Petowker to recite us the 'Blood-drinker's Burial' afterwards."

Everyone clapped their hands and stamped their feet at this proposal, but Miss Petowker said, "You know I dislike doing anything professional at private parties."

"Oh but not here!" said Mrs. Kenwigs. "We are all so very friendly and pleasant that you might as well be going through it in your own room—besides the occasion."

"I can't resist that," interrupted Miss Petowker, "anything in my humble power I shall be delighted to do."

In reality Mrs. Kenwigs and Miss Petowker had arranged all the entertainment between them beforehand, but had settled that a little pressing on each side would look more natural. Then Miss Petowker hummed a tune, and Morleena danced, the soles of her shoes being as carefully chalked as if she were going on the tight rope. It was a very beautiful figure with a great deal of work for the arms, and gained much applause; and Miss Petowker observed that if she had such a child as that she would have her out at the opera instantly. Then Miss Petowker was entreated to begin her recitation, so she let down her back hair, and went through the performance with great spirit, and died raving mad in the arms of a bachelor friend who was to rush out and catch her at the words "in death expire," to the great delight of the audience and the terror of the little Kenwigses, who were nearly frightened into fits.

Mr. Noggs was just going to say that the punch was ready, when a knock at the door startled them all. Mrs. Kenwigs shrieked, thinking the baby had fallen out of bed.

But it was only a friend of Mr. Noggs, who lived upstairs, and who had come down to say that Mr. Noggs was wanted by two queer-looking people all covered with mud and rain.

Mr. Noggs hurried out, saying he would be back soon, and presently startled them all by rushing in, snatching up a candle and a tumbler of hot punch, and darting out again.

Now, it happened unfortunately that the tumbler of punch was the very one that Mr. Lillyvick was just going to lift to his lips, and the great man—the rich relation—who

had it in his power to make Morleena and her sisters heiresses —and whom everyone was most anxious to please—was offended.

Poor Mr. Kenwigs endeavored to soothe him, but only made matters worse by saying he didn't think such a little

thing would have put him out of temper; Mr. Lillyvick demanded his hat, and was only induced to remain by Mrs.
Kenwigs' tears and sobs, and the entreaties of all the little
girls and the company, combined with those of his nephew-
in-law.

"There, Kenwigs," said Mr. Lillyvick, "and let me tell
you, to show you how much out of temper I was, that if I
had gone away without another word it would have made
no difference respecting that pound or two which I shall
leave among your children when I die."

"Morleena Kenwigs," cried her mother, "go down on
your knees to your dear uncle, and beg him to love you all
his life through; for he's more an angel than a man and
I've always said so."

Just as all were happy again, everyone was startled by
a rapid succession of the loudest and shrillest shrieks, apparently coming from the room where the baby was asleep.
Mrs. Kenwigs immediately thought that a strange cat must
must have got in and sucked the baby's breath while the
girl was asleep, and made for the door, screaming dismally—

"My baby, my blessed, blessed, blessed, blessed baby!
My own darling, sweet, innocent Lillyvick! Let me
go-o-o-o."

Mr. Kenwigs rushed out, and was met at the door of
the bedroom by a young man with the baby (upside down)
in his arms, who came out so quickly that he knocked Mr.
Kenwigs down; handing the child to his mother, he said,
"Don't be alarmed, it's all out, it's all over—the little girl,
being tired, I suppose, fell asleep and set her hair on fire.
I heard her cries and ran up in time to prevent her setting
fire to anything else. The child is not hurt; I took it off the
bed myself and brought it here to convince you."

All were very grateful to the young man, and invited him to join the party, but he excused himself, saying he had just had a very tiring journey, and wished to return to his friend, Mr, Noggs.

After they had all talked over this last excitement, and discussed little Lillyvick's deliverer, the collector pulled out his watch and announced that it was nearly two o'clock, and as the poor children had been for some time obliged to keep their little eyes open with their little forefingers, the company took leave, declaring they had never spent such a delightful evening, and that they wished Mr. and Mrs. Kenwigs had a wedding-day once a week, and many more remarks of the same kind; while Mr. and Mrs. Kenwigs, highly delighted with the success of their party, thanked them all for coming, and hoped they had enjoyed themselves only half as much as they said they had.

The Toy-Maker and His Blind Daughter.

CALEB PLUMMER and his blind daughter lived alone in a little cracked nutshell of a house. They were toy-makers, and their house, which was so small that it might have been knocked to pieces with a hammer and carried away in a cart, was stuck like a toad-stool on to the premises of Messrs. Gruff & Tackleton, the toy merchants for whom they worked—the latter of whom was himself both Gruff and Tackleton in one.

I am saying that Caleb and his blind daughter lived here. I should say Caleb did; his daughter lived in an enchanted palace, which her father's love had created for her. She did not know that the ceilings were cracked, the plaster tumbling down, and the woodwork rotten; that everything was old and ugly and poverty-stricken about her, and that her father was a gray-haired, stooping old man, and the master for whom they worked a hard and brutal taskmaster; oh, dear no, she fancied a pretty, cosy, compact little home full of tokens of a kind master's care, a smart, brisk, gallant-looking father, and a handsome and noble-looking toy merchant who was an angel of goodness.

This was all Caleb's doing. When his blind daughter was a baby he had determined, in his great love and pity for her, that her deprivation should be turned into a blessing, and her life as happy as he could make it. And she was happy; everything about her she saw with her father's eyes, in the rainbow-colored light with which it was his care and pleasure to invest it.

Caleb and his daughter were at work together in their

usual working-room, which served them for their ordinary living-room, as well; and a strange place it was. There were houses in it, finished and unfinished, for dolls of all stations in life. Suburban tenements, for dolls of moderate means; kitchens and single apartments for dolls of the lower classes; capital town residences for dolls of high estate. Some of these establishments were already furnished according to estimate, with a view to the convenience of dolls of limited income; others could be fitted on the most expensive scale, at a moment's notice, from whole shelves of chairs and tables, sofas, bedsteads, and upholstery. The nobility and gentry and public in general, for whose accommodation these tenements were designed, lay here and there in baskets, staring straight up at the ceiling; but in signifying their degrees in society, and confining them to their respective stations (which experience shows to be lamentably difficult in real life), the makers of these dolls had far improved on nature, who is often froward and perverse; for they, not resting on such arbitrary marks as satin, cotton-print and bits of rag, had superadded striking personal differences which allowed of no mistake. Thus, the doll-lady of distinction had wax limbs of perfect symmetry; but only she and her compeers, the next grade in the social scale being made of leather; and the next, coarse linen stuff. As to the common people, they had just so many matches out of tinder-boxes for their arms and legs, and there they were—established in their sphere at once, beyond the possibility of getting out of it.

There were various other samples of his handicraft besides dolls in Caleb Plummer's room. There were Noah's Arks, in which the birds and beasts were an uncommonly tight fit, I assure you; though they could be crammed in,

anyhow, at the roof, and rattled and shaken into the small-
est compass. By a bold poetical license most of these
Noah's Arks had knockers on the doors; inconsistent
appendages, perhaps, as suggestive of morning callers and a
postman, yet a pleasant finish to the outside of the building.
There were scores of melancholy little carts, which, when
the wheels went round, performed most doleful music.
Many small fiddles, drums, and other instruments of torture;
no end of cannon, shields, swords, spears and guns. There
were little tumblers in red breeches, incessantly swarming up
high obstacles of red tape, and coming down, head first,
upon the other side ; and there were innumerable old gentlemen of respectable, not to say venerable, appearance,
insanely flying over horizontal pegs, inserted, for the purpose,
in their own street doors.   There were beasts of all sorts,
horses in particular, of every breed, from the spotted
barrel on four legs, with a small tippet for a mane, to the
thoroughbred rocker on his highest mettle.

"You were out in the rain last night in your beautiful
new great-coat," said Bertha.

"Yes, in my beautiful new great-coat," answered Caleb,
glancing to where a roughly-made garment of sackcloth was
hung up to dry.

"How glad I am you bought it, father."

"And of such a tailor! quite a fashionable tailor; a
bright blue cloth, with bright buttons; it's a deal too good a
coat for me."

"Too good!" cried the blind girl, stopping to laugh
and clap her hands—"as if anything was too good for my
handsome father, with his smiling face, and black hair, and
his straight figure; as if any thing could be too good for my
handsome father!"

10

"I'm half ashamed to wear it, though," said Caleb, watching the effect of what he said upon her brightening face; "upon my word. When I hear the boys and people say behind me, 'Halloa! Here's a swell!' I don't know which way to look. And when the beggar wouldn't go away last night; and, when I said I was a very common man, said 'No, your honor! Bless your honor, don't say that!' I was quite ashamed. I really felt as if I hadn't a right to wear it."

Happy blind girl! How merry she was in her exultation!

"I see you, father," she said, clasping her hands, "as plainly as if I had the eyes I never want when you are with me. A blue coat——"

"Bright blue," said Caleb.

"Yes, yes! Bright blue!" exclaimed the girl, turning up her radiant face; "the color I can just remember in the blessed sky! You told me it was blue before. A bright blue coat——"

"Made loose to the figure," suggested Caleb.

"Yes! loose to the figure!" cried the blind girl, laughing heartily; "and in it you, dear father, with your merry eye, your smiling face, your free step, and your dark hair; looking so young and handsome!"

"Halloa! Halloa!" said Caleb, "I shall be vain presently."

"I think you are already," cried the blind girl, pointing at him, in her glee. "I know you, father! Ha, ha, ha! I've found you out, you see!"

How different the picture in her mind from Caleb, as he sat observing her! She had spoken of his free step. She was right in that. For years and years he never once had crossed that threshold at his own slow pace, but with a footfall counterfeited for her ear, and never had he, when his heart was heaviest, forgotten the light tread that was to render hers so cheerful and courageous.

"There we are," said Caleb, falling back a pace or two to form the better judgment of his work; "as near the real thing as sixpen'orth of halfpence is to sixpence. What a pity that the whole front of the house opens at once! If there was only a staircase in it now, and regular doors to the rooms to go in at! but that's the worst of my calling. I'm always deluding myself, and swindling myself."

"You are speaking quite softly. You are not tired, father?"

"Tired," echoed Caleb, with a great burst of animation, "what should tire me, Bertha? *I* was never tired. What does it mean?"

To give the greater force to his words, he stopped himself in an imitation of two small stretching and yawning figures on the mantelshelf, who were represented as in one eternal state of weariness from the waist upwards, and hummed a bit of a song. It was a drinking song, something about a sparkling bowl; and he sang it with an air of a devil-may-care voice, that made his face a thousand times more meagre and more thoughtful than ever.

"What! you're singing, are you?" said Tackleton, putting his head in at the door. "Go it! *I* can't sing."

Nobody would have suspected him of it. He hadn't what is generally termed a singing face, by any means.

"I can't afford to sing," said Tackleton. "I'm glad you can. I hope you can afford to work, too. Hardly time for both, I should think."

"If you could only see him, Bertha, how he's winking

at me!" whispered Caleb. "Such a man to joke! You'd
think, if you didn't know him, he was in earnest, wouldn't
you, now?"

The blind girl smiled and nodded.

"I am thanking you for the little tree, the beautiful little
tree," replied Bertha, bringing forward a tiny rose-tree in
blossom, which, by an innocent deception, Caleb had made
her believe was her master's gift, though he himself had
gone without a meal or two to buy it.

"The bird that can sing and won't sing must be made
to sing, they say," grumbled Tackleton. "What about the
owl that can't sing, and oughtn't to sing, and will sing; is
there anything that he should be made to do?"

"The extent to which he's winking at this moment!"
whispered Caleb to his daughter. "Oh, my gracious!"

"Always merry and light-hearted with us!" cried the
smiling Bertha.

"Oh! you're there, are you?" answered Tackleton.
"Poor idiot!"

He really did believe she was an idiot; and he founded
the belief, I can't say whether consciously or not, upon her
being fond of him.

"Well! and being there—how are you?" said Tackleton,
in his grudging way.

"Oh! well; quite well. And as happy as even you can
wish me to be. As happy as you would make the whole
world, if you could!"

"Poor idiot!" muttered Tackleton. "No gleam of
reason! Not a gleam!"

The blind girl took his hand and kissed it; held it for
a moment in her own two hands; and laid her cheek against
it tenderly, before releasing it. There was such unspeakable

affection and such fervent gratitude in the act, that Tackleton himself was moved to say, in a milder growl than usual;

"What's the matter now?"

"Bertha," said Tackleton, assuming, for once, a little cordiality. "Come here!"

"Oh! I can come straight to you. You needn't guide me," she rejoined.

"Shall I tell you a secret, Bertha?"

"If you will," she answered, eagerly.

How bright the darkened face! How adorned with light the listening head!

"This is the day on which little what's-her-name, the spoilt child, Peerybingle's wife, pays her regular visit to you—makes her fantastic picnic here, ain't it?" said Tackleton, with a strong expression of distaste for the whole concern.

"Yes," replied Bertha. "This is the day."

"I thought so," said Tackleton. "I should like to join the party."

"Do you hear that, father?" cried the blind girl in an ecstasy.

"Yes, yes, I hear it," murmured Caleb, with the fixed look of a sleep-walker; "but I do not believe it. It's one of my lies, I've no doubt."

"You see I—I want to bring the Peerybingles a little more into company with May Fielding," said Tackleton. "I am going to be married to May."

"Married!" cried the blind girl, starting from him.

"She's such a confounded idiot," muttered Tackleton, "that I was afraid she'd never comprehend me. Yes, Bertha, married. Church, parson, clerk, beadle, glass-coach, bells, breakfast, bride-cake, favors, marrow-bones, cleavers, and all the rest of the tomfoolery. A wedding, you know; a wedding. Don't you know what a wedding is?"

"I know," replied the blind girl, in a gentle tone. "I understand."

"Do you?" muttered Tackleton. "It's more than I expected. Well, on that account I want you to join the party, and to bring May and her mother. I'll send a little something or other, before the afternoon. A cold leg of mutton, or some comfortable trifle of that sort. You'll ex-pect me?"

"Yes," she answered.

She had drooped her head, and turned away; and so stood, with her hands crossed, musing.

"I don't think you will," muttered Tackleton, looking at her; "for you seem to have forgotten all about it already. Caleb!"

"I may venture to say I'm here, I suppose," thought Caleb. "Sir?"

"Take care she don't forget what I've been saying to her."

"*She* never forgets," returned Caleb. "It's one of the few things she ain't clever in."

"Every man thinks his own geese swans," observed the toy merchant, with a shrug. "Poor devil!"

Having delivered himself of which remark with infinite contempt, old Gruff & Tackleton withdrew.

Bertha remained where he had left her, lost in medita-tion. The gaiety had vanished from her downcast face, and it was very sad. Three or four times she shook her head, as if bewailing some remembrance or some loss; but her sorrowful reflections found no vent in words.

"Father, I am lonely in the dark. I want my eyes; my patient, willing eyes."

THE TOYMAKER AND HIS BLIND DAUGHTER

"Here they are," said Caleb. "Always ready. They are more yours than mine, Bertha, any hour in the four-and-twenty. What shall your eyes do for you, dear?"

"Look round the room, father."

"All right," said Caleb. "No sooner said than done, Bertha."

"Tell me about it."

"It's much the same as usual," said Caleb. "Homely, but very snug. The gay colors on the walls; the bright flowers on the plates and dishes; the shining wood, where there are beams or panels; the general cheerfulness and neatness of the building, make it very pretty."

Cheerful and neat it was, wherever Bertha's hands could busy themselves. But nowhere else were cheerfulness possible, in the old crazy shed which Caleb's fancy so transformed.

"You have your working dress on, and are not so gallant as when you wear the handsome coat," said Bertha, touching him.

"Not quite so gallant," answered Caleb. "Pretty brisk, though."

"Father," said the blind girl, drawing close to his side and stealing one arm round his neck, "tell me something about May. She is very fair?"

"She is, indeed," said Caleb. And she was indeed. It was quite a rare thing to Caleb not to have to draw on his invention.

"Her hair is dark," said Bertha, pensively, "darker than mine. Her voice is sweet and musical, I know. I have often loved to hear it. Her shape——"

"There's not a doll's in all the room to equal it," said Caleb "And her eyes——"

He stopped; for Bertha had drawn closer round his neck ; and, from the arm that clung about him, came a warning pressure which he understood too well.

He coughed a moment, hammered for a moment, and then fell back upon the song about the sparkling bowl; his infallible resource in all such difficulties.

"Our friend, father; our benefactor. I am never tired, you know, of hearing about him. Now was I, ever? she said, hastily.

"Of course not," answered Caleb. "And with reason."

"Ah! with how much reason?" cried the blind girl, with such fervency that Caleb, though his motives were pure, could not endure to meet her face, but dropped his eyes, as if she could have read in them his innocent deceit.

"Then tell me again about him, dear father," said Bertha. "Many times again. His face is benevolent, kind and tender. Honest and true, I am sure it is. The manly heart that tries to cloak all favors with a show of roughness and unwillingness beats in its every look and glance."

"And makes it noble," added Caleb in his quiet desperation.

"And makes it noble!" cried the blind girl. "He is older than May, father?"

"Ye-es," said Caleb, reluctantly. "He's a little older than May, but that don't signify."

"Bertha," said Caleb softly, "what has happened? How changed you are, my darling, in a few hours—since this morning. You silent and dull all day! What is it? Tell me!"

"Oh father, father!" cried the blind girl, bursting into tears. "Oh, my hard, hard fate!"

Caleb drew his hand across his eyes before he answered her.

"But think how cheerful and how happy you have been, Bertha. How good, and how much loved, by many people."

"That strikes me to the heart, dear father! Always so mindful of me! Always so kind to me!"

Caleb was very much perplexed to understand her.

"To be—to be blind, Bertha, my poor dear," he faltered, "is a great affliction; but——"

"I have never felt it!" cried the blind girl. "I have never felt it in its fullness. Never! I have sometimes wished that I could see you, or could see him; only once, dear father; only for one little minute. But, father! Oh, my good, gentle father, bear with me, if I am wicked!" said the blind girl. "This is not the sorrow that so weighs me down!"

"Bertha, my dear," said Caleb, "I have something on my mind I want to tell you, while we are alone. Hear me kindly. I have a confession to make to you, my darling."

"A confession, father?"

"I have wandered from the truth and lost myself, my child," said Caleb, with a pitiable expression in his bewildered face. "I have wandered from the truth, intending to be kind to you; and have been cruel."

She turned her wonder-stricken face towards him, and repeated, "Cruel! He cruel to me!" cried Bertha, with a smile of incredulity.

"Not meaning it, my child," said Caleb. "But I have been; though I never suspected it till yesterday. My dear, blind daughter, hear me and forgive me! The world you live in, heart of mine, doesn't exist as I have represented it. The eyes you have trusted in have been false to you.

She turned her wonder-stricken face towards him still.

"Your road in life was rough, my poor one," said Caleb, "and I meant to smooth it for you. I have altered objects, invented many things that never have been, to make you happier. I have had concealments from you, put deceptions on you, God forgive me! and surrounded you with fancies."

"But living people are not fancies," she said hurriedly, and turning very pale, and still retiring from him. "You can't change them."

"I have done so, Bertha," pleaded Caleb. "There is one person that you know, my Dove——"

"Oh, father! why do you say I know?" she answered in a tone of keen reproach. "What and whom do I know! I, who have no leader! I, so miserably blind!"

In the anguish of her heart she stretched out her hands, as if she were groping her way; then spread them, in a manner most forlorn and sad, upon her face.

"The marriage that takes place today," said Caleb, "is with a stern, sordid grinding man. A hard master to you and me, my dear, for many years. Ugly in his looks and in his nature. Cold and callous always. Unlike what I have painted him to you in everything, my child; in everything."

"Oh, why," cried the blind girl, tortured, as it seemed, almost beyond endurance, "why did you ever do this? Why did you ever fill my heart so full, and then come in, like death, and tear away the objects of my love? Oh, heaven, how blind I am! How helpless and alone!"

Her afflicted father hung his head, and offered no reply but in his penitence and sorrow.

"Tell me what my home is. What it truly is."

"It is a poor place, Bertha; very poor and bare indeed.

The house will scarcely keep out wind and rain another winter. It is as roughly shielded from the weather, Bertha, as your poor father in his sackcloth coat."

"Those presents that I took such care of, that came almost at my wish, and were so dearly welcome to me," she said, trembling; "where did they come from?"

Caleb did not answer. She knew already, and was silent.

'I see, I understand," said Bertha, "and now I am looking at you, at my kind, loving, compassionate father, tell me what is he like?"

"An old man, my child; thin, bent, gray-haired, worn-out with hard work and sorrow; a weak, foolish, deceitful old man."

The blind girl threw herself on her knees before him, and took his gray head in her arms. "It is my sight, it is my sight restored," she cried. "I have been blind, but now I see; I have never till now truly seen my father. Does he think that there is a gallant, handsome father in this earth that I could love so dearly, cherish so devotedly, as this worn and gray-headed old man? Father, there is not a gray hair on your head that shall be forgotten in my prayers and thanks to heaven."

"My Bertha!" sobbed Caleb, "and the brisk smart father in the blue coat—he's gone, my child."

"Dearest father, no, he's not gone, nothing is gone, everything I loved and believed in is here in this worn, old father of mine, and more—oh, so much more, too! I have been happy and contented, but I shall be happier and more contented still, now that I know what you are. I am *not* blind, father, any longer"

Little David Copperfield.

DAVID COPPERFIELD AND HIS MOTHER.

I, LITTLE DAVID COPPERFIELD, lived with my mother in a pretty house in the village of Blunderstone in Suffolk. I had never known my father, who died before I could remember anything, and I had neither brothers nor sisters. I was fondly loved by my pretty young mother, and our kind, good servant, Peggotty, and was a very happy little fellow. We had very few friends, and the only relation my mother talked about was an aunt of my father's, a tall and rather terrible old lady, from all accounts, who had once been to see us when I was quite a tiny baby, and had been so angry to find I was not a little girl that she had left the house quite offended, and had never been heard of since. One visitor, a tall, dark gentleman, I did not like at all, and was rather inclined to be jealous that my mother should be so friendly with the stranger.

Peggotty and I were sitting one night by the parlor fire, alone. I had been reading to Peggotty about crocodiles. I was tired of reading, and dead sleepy; but having leave, as a high treat, to sit up until my mother came home from spending the evening at a neighbor's, I would rather have died upon my post (of course) than have gone to bed. I had reached that stage of sleepiness when Peggotty seemed to swell and grow immensely large. I propped my eyelids open with my two forefingers, and looked perseveringly at her as she sat at work; at the little house with a thatched roof, where the yard-measure lived; at her work-box with a sliding-lid, with a view of St. Paul's Cathedral (with a pink dome) painted on the top; at the brass thimble on her finger; at herself, whom I thought lovely. I felt so sleepy that I knew if I lost sight of anything, for a moment, I was gone.

"Peggotty," says I, suddenly, "were you ever married?"

"Lord, Master Davy!" replied Peggotty. "What's put marriage in your head?"

She answered with such a start that it quite awoke me. And then she stopped in her work and looked at me, with her needle drawn out to its thread's length.

"But *were* you ever married, Peggotty?" says I. "You are a very handsome woman, ain't you?"

"Me handsome, Davy!" said Peggotty. "Lawk, no, my dear! But what put marriage in your head?"

"I don't know. You mustn't marry more than one person at a time, may you, Peggotty?"

"Certainly not," says Peggotty, with the promptest decision.

"But if you marry a person, and the person dies, why then you may marry another person, mayn't you, Peggotty?"

"You MAY," says Peggotty, "if you choose, my dear, That's a matter of opinion."

"But what is your opinion, Peggotty?" said I.

I asked her and looked curiously at her, because she looked so curiously at me.

"My opinion is," said Peggotty, taking her eyes from me, after a little indecision, and going on with her work, "that I never was married myself, Master Davy, and that I don't expect to be. That's all I know about the sub-ject."

"You ain't cross, I suppose, Peggotty, are you?" said I, after sitting quiet for a minute.

I really thought she was, she had been so short with me; but I was quite mistaken; for she laid aside her work (which was a stocking of her own) and opening her arms wide, took my curly head within them, and gave it a good squeeze. I know it was a good squeeze, because, being very plump, whenever she made any little exertion after she was dressed some of the buttons on the back of her gown flew off. And I recollect two bursting to the opposite side of the parlor, while she was hugging me.

One day Peggotty asked me if I would like to go with her on a visit to her brother at Yarmouth.

"Is your brother an agreeable man, Peggotty?" I inquired.

"Oh, what an agreeable man he is!" cried Peggotty. "Then there's the sea, and the boats and ships, and the fishermen, and the beach. And 'Am to play with."

Ham was her nephew. I was quite anxious to go when I heard of all these delights; but my mother, what would she do all alone? Peggotty told me my mother was going to pay a visit to some friends, and would be sure to let me go. So all was arranged, and we were to start the next day in the carrier's cart. I was so eager that I wanted to put my hat and coat on the night before! But when the time came to say good-bye to my dear mamma I cried a little, for I had never left her before. It was a rather slow way of traveling, and I was very tired and sleepy when I arrived at Yarmouth, and found Ham waiting to meet me. He was a great strong fellow, six feet high, and took me on his back and the box under his arm to carry both to the house. I was delighted to find that this house was made of a real, big, black boat, with a door and windows cut in the side, and an iron funnel sticking out of the roof for a chimney. Inside it was very cozy and clean, and I had a tiny bedroom in the stern. I was very much pleased to find a dear little girl, about my own age, to play with, and after tea I said:

"Mr. Peggotty."

"Sir," says he.

"Did you give your son the name of Ham because you lived in a sort of ark?"

Mr. Peggotty seemed to think it a deep idea, but answered:

"No, sir. I never giv' him no name.'

"Who gave him that name, then?" said I, putting question number two of the catechism to Mr. Peggotty.

"Why, sir, his father giv' it him," said Mr Peggotty.

"I thought you were his father."

"My brother Joe was *his* father," said Mr. Peggotty.

"Dead, Mr. Peggotty?" I hinted, after a respectful pause.

"Drowndead," said Mr. Peggotty.

I was very much surprised that Mr. Peggotty was not Ham's father, and began to wonder whether I was mistaken about his relationship to anybody else there. I was so curious to know that I made up my mind to have it out with Mr. Peggotty.

"Little Em'ly," I said, glancing at her. "She is your daughter, isn't she, Mr. Peggotty?"

"No, sir. My brother-in law, Tom, was *her* father."

I couldn't help it. "——Dead, Mr. Peggotty?" I hinted, after another respectful silence.

"Drowndead," said Mr. Peggotty.

I felt the difficulty of resuming the subject, but had not got to the bottom of it yet, and must get to the bottom somehow. So I said:

"Haven't you *any* children, Mr. Peggotty?"

"No, master," he answered, with a short laugh. "I'm a bacheldore."

"A bachelor!" I said, astonished. "Why, who's that, Mr. Peggotty?" pointing to the person in the apron who was knitting.

"That's Missis Gummidge," said Mr. Peggotty.

"Gummidge, Mr. Peggotty?"

But at this point Peggotty—I mean my own Peggotty— made such impressive motions to me not to ask any more questions that I could only sit and look at all the company, until it was time to go to bed.

Mrs. Gummidge lived with them, too, and did the cooking and cleaning, for she was a poor widow and had no home of her own. I thought Mr. Peggotty was very good to take all these people to live with him, and I was quite right, for Mr. Peggotty was only a poor man himself and had to work hard to get a living.

Almost as soon as morning shone upon the oyster-shell frame of my mirror I was out of bed, and out with little Em'ly picking up stones upon the beach.

"You're quite a sailor, I suppose?" I said to Em'ly. I don't know that I supposed anything of the kind, but I felt

DAVID COPPERFIELD AND LITTLE EM'LY

it an act of gallantry to say something; and a shining sail close to us made such a pretty little image of itself, at the moment, in her bright eye, that it came into my head to say this.

"No," replied Em'ly, shaking her head, "I'm afraid of the sea."

"Afraid!" I said, with a becoming air of boldness, and looking very big at the mighty ocean. "*I* ain't."

"Ah! but it's cruel," said Em'ly. "I have seen it very cruel to some of our men. I have seen it tear a boat as big as our house all to pieces."

"I hope it wasn't the boat that——"

"That father was drowned in?" said Em'ly. "No. Not that one. I never see that boat."

"Nor him?" I asked her.

Little Em'ly shook her head. 'Not to remember."

Here was a coincidence! I immediately went into an explanation how I had never seen my own father; and how my mother and I had always lived by ourselves in the happiest state imaginable, and lived so then, and always meant to live so; and how my father's grave was in the churchyard near our house, and shaded by a tree, beneath the boughs of which I had walked and heard the birds sing many a pleasant morning. But there were some differences between Em'ly's orphanhood and mine, it appeared. She had lost her mother before her father, and where her father's grave was no one knew, except that it was somewhere in the depths of the sea.

"Besides," said Em'ly, as she looked about for shells and pebbles, "your father was a gentleman and your mother is a lady; and my father was a fisherman and my mother was a fisherman's daughter, and my Uncle Dan is a fisherman."

"Dan is Mr. Peggotty, is he?" said I.

11

"Uncle Dan—yonder," answered Em'ly, nodding at the boat-house.

"Yes. I mean him. He must be very good, I should think."

"Good?" said Em'ly. "If I was ever to be a lady I'd give him a sky-blue coat with diamond buttons, nankeen trousers, a red velvet waistcoat, a cocked hat, a large gold watch, a silver pipe and a box of money."

I said I had no doubt that Mr. Peggotty well deserved these treasures.

Little Em'ly had stopped and looked up at the sky in her enumeration of these articles, as if they were a glorious vision. We went on again, picking up shells and pebbles.

"You would like to be a lady?" I said.

Em'ly looked at me, and laughed and nodded "yes."

"I should like it very much. We would all be gentle-folks together, then. Me, and uncle, and Ham, and Mrs. Gummidge. We wouldn't mind then, when there come stormy weather. Not for our own sakes, I mean. We would for the poor fishermen's, to be sure, and we'd help 'em with money when they come to any hurt."

I was quite sorry to leave these kind people and my dear little companion, but still I was glad to think that I should get back to my own dear mamma. When I reached home, however, I found a great change. My mother was married to the dark man I did not like, whose name was Mr. Murdstone, and he was a stern, hard man, who had no love for me, and did not allow my mother to pet and indulge me as she had done before. Mr. Murdstone's sister came to live with us, and as she was even more difficult to please than her brother, and disliked boys, my life was no longer a happy one. I tried to be good and obedient, for I knew it made my mother very unhappy to see me punished and found fault with. I had always had lessons with my mother, and as she was patient and gentle I had enjoyed learning to read, but now I had a great many very hard lessons to do, and was so frightened and shy when Mr. and Miss Murdstone were in the room, that I did not get on at all well, and was continually in disgrace.

Let me remember how it used to be, and bring one morning back again.

I come into the second-best parlor after breakfast, with my books, and an exercise-book and a slate. My mother is ready for me at her writing-desk, but not half so ready as Mr. Murdstone in his easy-chair by the window (though he pretends to be reading a book), or as Miss Murdstone, sitting near my mother stringing steel beads. The very sight of these two has such an influence over me that I begin to feel the words I have been at infinite pains to get into my head all sliding away, and going, I don't know where. I wonder where they *do* go, by-the-by?

I hand the first book to my mother. Perhaps it is a grammar, perhaps a history, or geography. I take a last drowning look at the page as I give it into her hand, and start off aloud at a racing pace while I have got it fresh. I trip over a word. Mr. Murdstone looks up. I trip over another word. Miss Murdstone looks up. I redden, tumble over half a dozen words, and stop. I think my mother would show me the book if she dared, but she does not dare, and she says softly:

"Oh, Davy, Davy!"

"Now, Clara," says Mr. Murdstone, "be firm with the boy. Don't say, Oh, Davy, Davy!' That's childish. He knows his lesson, or he does not know it."

"He does *not* know it," Miss Murdstone interposes awfully.

"I am really afraid he does not," says my mother.

"Then you see, Clara," returns Miss Murdstone, "you should just give him the book back, and make him know it."

"Yes, certainly," says my mother; "that is what I in-tend to do, my dear Jane. Now, Davy, try once more, and don't be stupid."

I obey the first clause of the injunction by trying once more, but am not so successful with the second, for I am very stupid. I tumble down before I get to the old place, at a point where I was all right before, and stop to think. But I can't think about the lesson. I think of the number of yards of net in Miss Murdstone's cap, or of the price of Mr. Murdstone's dressing-gown, or any such ridiculous problem that I have no business with, and don't want to have anything at all to do with. Mr. Murdstone makes a movement of impatience which I have been expecting for a long time. Miss Murdstone does the same. My mother glances submissively at them, shuts the book, and lays it by as an arrear to be worked out when my other tasks are done.

There is a pile of these arrears very soon, and it swells like a rolling snowball. The bigger it gets, the more stupid I get. The case is so hopeless, and I feel that I am wallowing in such a bog of nonsense, that I give up all idea of getting out, and abandon myself to my fate. The despairing way in which my mother and I look at each other, as I blunder on, is truly melancholy. But the great-est effect in these miserable lessons is when my mother (thinking nobody is observing her) tries to give me the cue by the motion of her lips. At that instant, Miss Murdstone, who has been lying in wait for nothing else all along, says in a deep warning voice:

"Clara!"

My mother starts, colors and smiles faintly.   Mr. Murdstone comes out of his chair, takes the book, throws it at me, or boxes my ears with it, and turns me out of the room by the shoulders.

My only pleasure was to go up into a little room at the top of the house where I had found a number of books that had belonged to my own father, and I would sit and read Robinson Crusoe, and many tales of travels and adventures, and I imagined myself to be sometimes one and sometimes another hero, and went about for days with the centre-piece out of an old set of boot-trees, pretending to be a captain in the British Royal Navy.

One morning when I went into the parlor with my books, I found my mother looking anxious, Miss Murdstone looking firm, and Mr. Murdstone binding something round the bottom of a cane—a lithe and limber cane, which he left off binding when I came in, and poised and switched in the air.

"I tell you, Clara," said Mr. Murdstone, "I have often been flogged myself."

"To be sure; of course," said Miss Murdstone.

"Certainly, my dear Jane," faltered my mother, meekly. "But—but do you think it did Edward good?"

"Do you think it did Edward harm, Clara?" asked Mr. Murdstone, gravely.

"That's the point!" said his sister.

To this my mother returned, "Certainly, my dear Jane," and said no more.

I felt apprehensive that I was personally interested in

this dialogue, and sought Mr. Murdstone's eye as it lighted
on mine.

"Now, David," he said—and I saw that cast again, as
he said it—"you must be far more careful to-day than usual."
He gave the cane another poise and another switch; and
having finished his preparation of it, laid it down beside
him, with an expressive look, and took up his book.

This was a good freshener to my presence of mind, sa
a beginning. I felt the words of my lessons slipping off,
not one by one, or line by line, but by the entire page. I
tried to lay hold of them; but they seemed, if I may so express it, to have put skates on, and to skim away from me
with a smoothness there was no checking.

We began badly, and went on worse. I had come in
with an idea of distinguishing myself rather, conceiving that
I was very well prepared; but it turned out to be quite a
mistake. Book after book was added to the heap of failures,
Miss Murdstone being firmly watchful of us all the time.
And when we came at last to the five thousand cheeses
(canes he made it that day, I remember), my mother burst
out crying.

"Clara!" said Miss Murdstone, in her warning voice.

"I am not quite well, my dear Jane, I think," said my
mother.

I saw him wink, solemnly, at his sister, as he rose and
said, taking up the cane:

"Why, Jane, we can hardly expect Clara to bear, with
perfect firmness, the worry and torment that David has oc-
casioned her to-day. Clara is greatly strengthened and improved, but we can hardly expect so much from her. David,
you and I will go upstairs, boy."

As he took me out at the door, my mother ran towards

us. Miss Murdstone said, "Clara! are you a perfect fool?" and interfered. I saw my mother stop her ears then, and I heard her crying.

He walked me up to my room slowly and gravely—I am certain he had a delight in that formal parade of executing justice—and when we got there, suddenly twisted my head under his arm.

"Mr. Murdstone! Sir!" I cried to him. "Don't! Pray don't beat me! I have tried to learn, sir, but I can't learn while you and Miss Murdstone are by. I can't, indeed!"

"Can't you, indeed, David?" he said. "We'll try that."

He had my head as in a vise, but I twined round him somehow, and stopped him for a moment, entreating him not to beat me. It was only for a moment that I stopped him, for he cut me heavily an instant, afterwards, and in the same instant I caught the hand with which he held me in my mouth, between my teeth, and bit it through. It sets my teeth on edge to think of it.

He beat me then, as if he would have beaten me to death. Above all the noise we made, I heard them running up the stairs, and crying out—I heard my mother crying out —and Peggotty. Then he was gone; and the door was locked outside; and I was lying, fevered and hot, and torn, and sore, and raging in my puny way, upon the floor.

How well I recollect, when I became quiet, what an unnatural stillness seemed to reign through the whole house! How well I remember, when my smart and passion began to cool, how wicked I began to feel!

I sat listening for a long while, but there was not a sound. I crawled up from the floor, and saw my face in the glass, so swollen, red and ugly that it almost frightened me. My stripes were sore and stiff, and made me cry afresh, when

I moved; but they were nothing to the guilt I felt. It lay heavier on my breast than if I had been a most atrocious criminal, I dare say.

It had begun to grow dark, and I had shut the window (I had been lying, for the most part, with my head upon the sill, by turns crying, dozing and looking listlessly out), when the key was turned, and Miss Murdstone came in with some bread and meat and milk. These she put down upon the table without a word, glaring at me the while with exemplary firmness, and then retired, locking the door after her.

I never shall forget the waking, next morning; the being cheerful and fresh for the first moment, and then the being weighed down by the stale and dismal oppression of remembrance. Miss Murdstone reappeared before I was out of bed; told me, in so many words, that I was free to walk in the garden for half an hour and no longer; and retired, leaving the door open, that I might avail myself of that permission.

I did so, and did so every morning of my imprisonment, which lasted five days. If I could have seen my mother alone, I should have gone down on my knees to her and besought her forgiveness; but I saw no one, Miss Murdstone excepted, during the whole time.

The length of those five days I can convey no idea of to anyone. They occupy the place of years in my remembrance.

On the last night of my restraint, I was awakened by hearing my own name spoken in a whisper. I started up in bed, and, putting out my arms in the dark, said:

"Is that you, Peggotty?"

There was no immediate answer, but presently I heard my name again, in a tone so very mysterious and awful, that I think I should have gone into a fit, if it had not occurred to me that it must have come through the keyhole.

I groped my way to the door, and, putting my own lips to the keyhole, whispered :

"Is that you, Peggotty, dear?"

"Yes, my own precious Davy," she replied. "Be as soft as a mouse, or the cat'll hear us."

I understood this to mean Miss Murdstone, and was sensible of the urgency of the case; her room being close by.

"How's mamma, dear Peggotty? Is she very angry with me?

I could hear Peggotty crying softly on her side of the keyhole, as I was doing on mine, before she answered. "No. Not very."

"What is going to be done with me, Peggotty, dear? Do you know?"

"School. Near London," was Peggotty's answer. I was obliged to get her to repeat it, for she spoke it the first time quite down my throat in consequence of my having forgotten to take my mouth away from the keyhole and put my ear there ; and, though her words tickled me a good deal, I didn't hear them.

"When, Peggotty?"

"To-morrow."

"Is that the reason why Miss Murdstone took the clothes out of my drawers?" which she had done, though I had forgotten to mention it.

"Yes," said Peggotty. "Box."

"Shan't I see mamma?"

"Yes," said Peggotty. "Morning."

Then Peggotty fitted her mouth close to the keyhole, and delivered these words through it with as much feeling and earnestness as a keyhole has ever been the medium of communicating, I will venture to assert, shooting in each broken little sentence in a convulsive little burst of its own.

"Davy, dear. If I ain't been azackly as intimate with you. Lately, as I used to be. It ain't because I don't love you. Just as well and more, my pretty poppet. It's because I thought it better for you. And for someone else besides. Davy, my darling, are you listening? Can you hear?"

"Ye—ye—ye—yes, Peggotty," I sobbed.

"My own!" said Peggotty, with infinite compassion. "What I want to say, is. That you must never forget me. For I'll never forget you. And I'll take as much care of your mamma, Davy. As I ever took of you. And I won't leave her. The day may come when she'll be glad to lay her poor head. On her stupid, cross old Peggotty's arm again. And I'll write to you, my dear. Though I ain't no scholar. And I'll—I'll—" Peggotty fell to kissing the keyhole, as she couldn't kiss me.

"Thank you, dear Peggotty," said I. "Oh, thank you! Thank you! Will you promise me one thing, Peggotty? Will you write and tell Mr. Peggotty and little Em'ly and Mrs. Gummidge and Ham that I am not so bad as they might suppose, and that I sent 'em all my love—especially to little Em'ly? Will you, if you please, Peggotty?"

The kind soul promised, and we both of us kissed the keyhole with the greatest affection—I patted it with my hand, I recollect, as if it had been her honest face—and parted.

In the morning Miss Murdstone appeared as usual, and told me I was going to school; which was not altogether such news to me as she supposed. She also informed me that when I was dressed, I was to come downstairs into the parlor and have my breakfast. There I found my mother, very pale and with red eyes; into whose arms I ran, and begged her pardon from my suffering soul.

"Oh Davy!" she said. "That you could hurt anyone I love! Try to be better, pray to be better! I forgive you; but I am so grieved, Davy, that you should have such bad passions in your heart."

Miss Murdstone was good enough to take me out to the cart, and to say on the way that she hoped I would repent, before I came to a bad end; and then I got into the cart, and the lazy horse walked off with it.

We might have gone about half a mile, and my pocket handkerchief was quite wet through, when the carrier stopped short.

Looking out to ascertain for what, I saw, to my amazement, Peggotty burst from a hedge and climb into the cart. She took me in both her arms and squeezed me until the pressure on my nose was extremely painful, though I never thought of that until afterwards, when I found it very tender. Not a single word did Peggotty speak. Releasing one of her arms, she put it down in her pocket to the elbow, and brought out some paper-bags of cakes, which she crammed into my pockets, and a purse which she put into my hand, but not one word did she say. After another and a final squeeze with both arms, she got down from the cart and ran away; and my belief is, and has always been, without a solitary button on her gown. I picked up one, of several that was rolling about, and treasured it as a keepsake for a long time.

The carrier looked at me, as if to enquire if she were coming back. I shook my head, and said I thought not. "Then come up!" said the carrier to the lazy horse, who came up accordingly.

Having by this time cried as much as I possibly could, I began to think it was of no use crying any more, especially as neither Roderick Random nor that captain in the Royal British Navy had ever cried, that I could remember, in trying situations. The carrier seeing me in this resolution, proposed that my pocket handkerchief should be spread upon the horse's back to dry. I thanked him and assented; and particularly small it looked under those circumstances.

I had now leisure to examine the purse. It was a stiff leather purse, with a snap, and had three bright shillings in it, which Peggotty had evidently polished up with whitening, for my greater delight. But its precious contents were two half-crowns folded together in a bit of paper, on which was written in my mother's hand, "For Davy. With my love." I was so overcome by this, that I asked the carrier to be so good as reach me my pocket handkerchief again, but he said he thought I had better do without it; and I thought I really had, so I wiped my eyes on my sleeve and stopped myself.

For good, too; though in consequence of my previous emotions, I was still occasionally seized with a stormy sob. After we had jogged on for some little time, I asked the carrier if he was going all the way.

"All the way where?" inquired the carrier.

"There," I said.

"Where's there?" inquired the carrier.

"Near London," I said.

"Why that horse," said the carrier, jerking the rein to point him out, "would be deader than pork afore he got over half the ground."

"Are you only going to Yarmouth then?" I asked.

"That's about it," said the carrier. "And there I

shall take you to the stage-cutch, and the stage-cutch that'll take you to—wherever it is."

I shared my cakes with the carrier, who asked if Peggotty made them and told him yes, she did all our cooking. The carrier looked thoughtful, and then asked if I would send a message to Peggotty from him. I agreed, and the message was "Barkis is willing." While I was waiting for the coach at Yarmouth, I wrote to Peggotty :

"MY DEAR PEGGOTTY :—I have come here safe. Barkis is willing. My love to mamma. Yours affectionately.

"P. S.—He says he particularly wanted you to know *Barkis is willing.*"

At Yarmouth I found dinner was ordered for me, and felt very shy at having a table all to myself, and very much alarmed when the waiter told me had seen a gentleman fall down dead after drinking some of their beer. I said I would have some water, and was quite grateful to the waiter for drinking the ale that had been ordered for me, for fear the people of the hotel should be offended. He also helped me to eat my dinner, and accepted one of my bright shillings.

After a long, tiring journey by the coach, for there were no trains in those days, I arrived in London and was taken to the school at Blackheath by one of the masters, Mr. Mell.

I gazed upon the schoolroom into which he took me as the most forlorn and desolate place I had ever seen. I see it now. A long room, with three long rows of desks, and six of forms, and bristling all round with pegs for hats and slates. Scraps of old copy-books and exercises litter the dirty floor .

Mr. Mell having left me while he took his irreparable boots upstairs, I went softly to the upper end of the room,

observing all this as I crept along.   Suddenly I came upon
a pasteboard placard, beautifully written, which was lying
on the desk, and bore these words—"*Take care of him.
He bites.*

[LITTLE DAVID COPPERFIELD AND BARKIS.

I got upon the desk immediately, apprenhensive of at
least a great dog underneath. But, though I looked all
round with anxious eyes, I could see nothing of him. I was
still engaged in peering about when Mr. Mell came back,
and asked me what I did up there.

"I beg your pardon, sir," says I, "if you please, I'm looking for the dog."

"Dog," says he. "What dog?"

"Isn't it a dog, sir?"

"Isn't what a dog?"

"That's to be taken care of, sir; that bites."

"No, Copperfield," says he, gravely, "that's not a dog. That's a boy. My instructions are, Copperfield, to put this placard on your back. I am sorry to make such a beginning with you, but I must do it."

With that, he took me down, and tied the placard, which was neatly constructed for the purpose, on my shoulders like a knapsack; and wherever I went, afterwards, I had the consolation of carrying it.

What I suffered from that placard, nobody can imagine. Whether it was possible for people to see me or not, I always fancied that somebody was reading it. It was no relief to turn round and find nobody; for wherever my back was, there I imagined somebody always to be.

There was an old door in this playground, on which the boys had a custom of carving their names. It was completely covered with such inscriptions. In my dread of the end of the vacation and their coming back, I could not read one boy's name, without inquiring in what tone and with what emphasis *he* would read, "Take care of him. He bites." There was one boy—a certain J. Steerforth—who cut his name very deep and very often, who, I conceived, would read it in a rather strong voice, and afterwards pull my hair. There was another boy, one Tommy Traddles, who I dreaded would make game of it, and pretend to be dreadfully frightened of me. There was a third, George Demple, who I fancied would sing it. I have looked, a

little shrinking creature, at that door, until the owners of all
the names—there were five-and-forty of them in the school
then, Mr. Mell said—seemed to send me to Coventry by
general acclamation, and to cry out, each in his own way,
"Take care of him. He bites!"

Tommy Traddles was the first boy who returned. He
introduced himself by informing me that I should find his
name on the right-hand corner of the gate, over the top bolt;
upon that I said, "Traddles?" to which he replied, "The
same," and then he asked me for a full account of myself
and family.

It was a happy circumstance for me that Traddles came
back first. He enjoyed my placard so much that he saved
me from the embarrassment of either disclosure or concealment, by presenting me to every other boy who came back,
great or small, immediately on his arrival, in this form of
introduction, "Look here! Here's a game!" Happily, too,
the greater part of the boys came back low-spirited, and
were not so boisterous at my expense as I had expected.
Some of them certainly did dance about me like wild
Indians, and the greater part could not resist the temptation
of pretending that I was a dog, and patting and smoothing
me lest I should bite, and saying, "Lie down, sir!" and
calling me Towzer. This was naturally confusing, among
so many strangers, and cost me some tears, but on the
whole it was much better than I had anticipated.

I was not considered as being formally received into the
school, however, until J. Steerforth arrived. Before this
boy, who was reputed to be a great scholar, and was very
good-looking, and at least half-a-dozen years my senior, I
was carried as before a magistrate. He inquired, under a
shed in the playground, into the particulars of my punish-

ment, and was pleased to express his opinion that it was a
"jolly shame;" for which I became bound to him ever
afterwards.

"What money have you got, Copperfield?" he said,
walking aside with me when he had disposed of my affair in
these terms.

I told him seven shillings.

"You had better give it to me to take care of," he said.
"At least, you can, if you like. You needn't if you don't
like."

I hastened to comply with his friendly suggestion, and,
opening Peggotty's purse, turned it upside down into his
hand.

"Do you want to spend anything now?" he asked me.

"No, thank you," I replied.

"You can, if you like, you know," said Steerforth.
"Say the word."

"No, thank you, sir," I repeated.

"Perhaps you'd like to spend a couple of shillings or so
in a bottle of currant wine by-and-by, up in the bedroom?"
said Steerforth. "You belong to my bedroom, I find."

It certainly had not occurred to me before, but I said,
"Yes, I should like that."

"Very good," said Steerforth. "You'll be glad to
spend another shilling or so in almond cakes, I dare say?"

I said, "Yes, I should like that, too."

"And another shilling or so in biscuits, and another in
fruit, eh?" said Steerforth. "I say, young Copperfield,
you're going it!"

I smiled because he smiled, but I was a little troubled
in my mind, too.

"Well!" said Steerforth. "We must make it stretch

12

as far as we can; that's all. I'll do the best in my power
for you. I can go out when I like, and I'll smuggle the
prog in." With these words he put the money in his
pocket, and kindly told me not to make myself uneasy; he
would take care it should be all right

He was as good as his word, if that were all right
which I had a secret misgiving was nearly all wrong—for I
feared it was a waste of my mother's two half-crowns—
though I had preserved the piece of paper they were wrapped
in; which was a precious saving. When we went upstairs
to bed, he produced the whole seven shillings' worth, and
laid it out on my bed in the moonlight, saying:

"There you are, young Copperfield, and a royal spread
you've got!"

I couldn't think of doing the honors of the feast at my
time of life, while he was by; my hand shook at the very
thought of it. I begged him to do me the favor of presiding;
and my request being seconded by the other boys who were
in that room, he acceded to it, and sat upon my pillow,
handing round the viands—with perfect fairness, I must
say—and dispensing the currant wine in a little glass without
a foot, which was his own property. As to me, I sat on his
left hand, and the rest were grouped about us, on the nearest
beds and on the floor.

How well I recollect our sitting there, talking in
whispers; or their talking, and my respectfully listening, I
ought rather to say; the moonlight falling a little way into
the room, through the window, painting a pale window on
the floor, and the greater part of us in shadow, except when
Steerforth dipped a match into a phosphorus-box, when he
wanted to look for anything on the board, and shed a blue
glare over us that was gone directly. A certain mysterious

feeling, consequent on the darkness, the secrecy of the revel, and the whisper in which everything was said, steals over me again, and I listen to all they tell me, with a vague feeling of solemnity and awe, which makes me glad they are all so near, and frightens me (though I feign to laugh) when Traddles pretends to see a ghost in the corner.

I heard all kinds of things about the school and all belonging to it. I heard that Mr. Creakle was the sternest and most severe of masters; that he laid about him, right and left, every day of his life, charging in among the boys like a trooper, and slashing away, unmercifully.

I heard that the man with the wooden leg, whose name was Tungay, was an obstinate barbarian who had formerly assisted in the hop business, but had come into the line with Mr. Creakle, in consequence, as was supposed among the boys, of his having broken his leg in Mr. Creakle's service, and having done a deal of dishonest work for him, and knowing his secrets.

But the greatest wonder that I heard of Mr. Creakle was, there being one boy in the school on whom he never ventured to lay a hand, and that boy being J. Steerforth. Steerforth himself confirmed this when it was stated, and said that he should like to begin to see him do it. On being asked by a mild boy (not me) how he would proceed if he did begin to see him do it, he dipped a match into his phosphorus-box on purpose to shed a glare over his reply, and said he would commence with knocking him down with a blow on the forehead from the seven-and-six-penny ink-bottle that was always on the mantelpiece. We sat in the dark for some time, breathless.

I heard that Miss Creakle was regarded by the school in general as being in love with Steerforth; and I am sure, as

I sat in the dark, thinking of his nice voice, and his fine face, and his easy manner, and his curling hair, I thought it very likely.   I heard that Mr. Mell was not a bad sort of fellow, but hadn't a sixpence to bless himself with; and that there was no doubt that old Mrs. Mell, his mother, was as poor as Job.

One day, Traddles (the most unfortunate boy in the world) breaks a window accidentally with a ball.   I shudder at this moment with the tremendous sensation of seeing it done, and feeling that the ball has bounded on to Mr. Creakle's sacred head.

Poor Traddles!   In a tight sky-blue suit that made his arms and legs like German sausages, or roly-poly puddings, he was the merriest and most miserable of all the boys.   He was always being caned—I think he was caned every day that half-year, except one holiday Monday, when he was only rulered on both hands—and was always going to write to his uncle about it, and never did.   After laying his head on the desk for a little while, he would cheer up somehow, begin to laugh again, and draw skeletons all over his slate before his eyes were dry.   I used at first to wonder what comfort Traddles found in drawing skeletons.   But I believe he only did it because they were easy, and didn't want any features.

He was very honorable, Traddles was; and held it as a solemn duty in the boys to stand by one another.   He suffered for this on several occasions; and particularly once, when Steerforth laughed in church, and the beadle thought it was Traddles, and took him out.   I see him now, going away in custody, despised by the congregation.   He never said who was the real offender, though he smarted for it next day, and was imprisoned so many hours that he came forth with a whole churchyard full of skeletons swarming all over his

Latin Dictionary.   But he had his reward.   Steerforth said
there was nothing of the sneak in Traddles, and we all felt
that to be the highest praise.   For my part, I could have
gone through a great deal (though I was much less brave
than Traddles, and nothing like so old) to have won such a
recompense.

To see Steerforth walk to church before us, arm-in-arm
with Miss Creakle, was one of the great sights of my life.
I didn't think Miss Creakle equal to little Em'ly in point of
beauty, and I didn't love her (I didn't dare); but I thought
her a young lady of extraordinary attractions, and in point
of gentility not to be surpassed.   When Steerforth, in white
trousers, carried her parasol for her, I felt proud to know
him; and believed that she could not choose but adore him
with all her heart.   Mr. Sharp and Mr. Mell were both
notable personages in my eyes; but Steerforth was to them
what the sun was to two stars.

An accidental circumstance cemented the intimacy between Steerforth and me, in a manner that inspired me with
great pride and satisfaction, though it sometimes led to inconvenience.   It happened on one occasion, when he was
doing me the honor of talking to me in the playground, that
I hazarded the observation that something or somebody—I
forget what now—was like something or somebody in Peregrine Pickle.   He said nothing at the time; but when I was
going to bed at night, asked me if I had got that book.

I told him no, and explained how it was that I had read
it, and all those other books of which I had made mention.

"And do you recollect them?" Steerforth said.

"Oh, yes," I replied; I had a good memory, and I believed I recollected them very well.

"Then I tell you what, young Copperfield," said Stee

forth," you shall tell 'em to me. I can't get to sleep very
early at night, and I generally wake rather early in the
morning. We'll go over 'em one after another. We'll make
some regular Arabian Nights of it."

I felt extremely flattered by this arrangement, and we
commenced carrying it into execution that very evening.

Steerforth showed his consideration in one particular
instance; in an unflinching manner that was a little tantal-
izing, I suspect, to poor Traddles and the rest. Peggotty's
promised letter—what a comfortable letter it was!—arrived
before "the half" was many weeks old; and with it a cake
in a perfect nest of oranges, and two bottles of cowslip wine.
This treasure, as in duty bound, I laid at the feet of Steerforth, and begged him to dispense.

"Now, I'll tell you what, young Copperfield," said he,
"the wine shall be kept to wet your whistle when you are
story-telling."

I blushed at the idea, and begged him, in my modesty,
not to think of it. But he said he had observed I was sometimes hoarse—a little roopy was his exact expression—and
it should be, every drop, devoted to the purpose he had
mentioned. Accordingly, it was locked up in his box, and
drawn off by himself in a phial, and administered to me
through a piece of quill in the cork, when I was supposed to
be in want of a restorative. Sometimes, to make it a more
sovereign specific, he was so kind as to squeeze orange
juice into it, or to stir it up with ginger, or dissolve a peppermint drop in it.

We seem to me to have been months over Peregrine,
and months more over the other stories. The institution
never flagged for want of a story, I am certain; and the
wine lasted out almost as well as the matter. Poor Trad-

dles—I never think of that boy but with a strange disposition to laugh, and with tears in my eyes—was a sort of
chorus, in general; and affected to be convulsed with mirth
at the comic parts, and to be overcome with fear when there
was any passage of an alarming character in the narrative.
This rather put me out very often. It was a great jest of
his, I recollect, to pretend that he couldn't keep his teeth
from chattering, whenever mention was made of an Alguazil
in connection with the adventures of Gil Blas; and I remember when Gil Blas met the captain of the robbers in Madrid,
this unlucky joker counterfeited such an ague of terror that
he was overheard by Mr. Creakle, who was prowling about
the passage, and handsomely flogged for disorderly conduct
in the bedroom.

One day I had a visit from Mr. Peggotty and Ham, who
had brought two enormous lobsters, a huge crab, and a
large canvas bag of shrimps, as they "remembered I was
partial to a relish with my meals."

I was proud to introduce my friend Steerforth to these
kind, simple friends, and told them how good Steerforth
was to me, and how he helped me with my work and took
care of me, and Steerforth delighted the fishermen with his
friendly, pleasant manners.

The "relish" was much appreciated by the boys at supper that night. Only poor Traddles became very ill from
eating crab so late.

At last the holidays came, and I went home. The carrier, Barkis, met me at Yarmouth, and was rather gruff,
which I soon found out was because he had not had any
answer to his message. I promised to ask Peggotty for
one.

Ah, what a strange feeling it was to be going home

when it was not home, and to find that every object I locked at reminded me of the happy old home, which was like a dream I could never dream again!

God knows how infantine the memory may have been that was awakened within me by the sound of my mother's voice in the old parlor, when I set foot in the hall.

I believed, from the solitary and thoughtful way in which my mother murmured her song, that she was alone. And I went softly into the room. She was sitting by the fire, nursing an infant, whose tiny hand she held against her neck. Her eyes were looking down upon its face, and she sat singing to it. I was so far right, that she had no other companion.

I spoke to her, and she started, and cried out. But seeing me, she called me her dear Davy, her own boy; and coming half across the room to meet me, kneeled down upon the ground and kissed me, and laid my head down on her bosom near the little creature that was nestling there, and put its hand up to my lips.

I wish I had died. I wish I had died then, with that feeling in my heart! I should have been more fit for heaven than I ever have been since.

"He is your brother," said my mother, fondling me. "Davy, my pretty boy! My poor child!" Then she kissed me more and more, and clasped me round the neck. This she was doing when Peggotty came running in, and bounced down on the ground beside us and went mad about us both for a quarter of an hour.

We had a very happy afternoon the day I came. Mr. and Miss Murdstone were out, and I sat with my mother and Peggotty, and told them all about my school and Steerforth, and took the little baby in my arms and nursed it lovingly. But when the Murdstones came back I was more unhappy than ever.

I felt uncomfortable about going down to breakfast in the morning, as I had never set eyes on Mr. Murdstone since the day when I committed my memorable offense. However, as it must be done, I went down, after two or three false starts half-way, and as many runs back on tiptoe to my own room, and presented myself in the parlor.

He was standing before the fire with his back to it, while Miss Murdstone made the tea. He looked at me steadily as I entered, but made no sign of recognition whatever.

I went up to him, after a moment of confusion, and said, "I beg your pardon, sir. I am very sorry for what I did, and I hope you will forgive me."

"I am glad to hear you are sorry, David," he replied.

The hand he gave me was the hand I had bitten. I could not restrain my eye from resting for an instant on a red spot upon it.

"How do you do, ma'am?" I said to Miss Murdstone.

"Ah, dear me!" sighed Miss Murdstone, giving me the tea-caddy scoop instead of her fingers. "How long are the holidays?"

"A month, ma'am."

"Counting from when?"

"From to-day, ma'am."

"Oh!" said Miss Murdstone. "Then here's *one* day off."

She kept a calendar of the holidays in this way, and every morning checked a day off in exactly the same manner. She did it gloomily until she came to ten, but when she got into two figures she became more hopeful, and, as the time advanced, even jocular.

Thus the holidays lagged away, until the morning came when Miss Murdstone said: "Here's the last day off!" and gave me the closing cup of tea of the vacation.

I was not sorry to go. Again Mr. Barkis appeared at the gate, and again Miss Murdstone in her warning voice said: "Clara!" when my mother bent over me, to bid me farewell.

I kissed her and my baby brother; it is not so much the embrace she gave me that lives in my mind, though it was as fervent as could be, as what followed the embrace.

I was in the carrier's cart when I heard her calling to me. I looked out, and she stood at the garden gate alone, holding her baby up in her arms for me to see. It was cold, still weather; and not a hair of her head, or fold of her dress, was stirred, as she looked intently at me, holding up her child.

So I lost her. So I saw her afterwards, in my sleep at school—a silent presence near my bed—looking at me with the same intent face—holding up her baby in her arms.

About two months after I had been back at school I was sent for one day to go into the parlor. I hurried joy-fully, for it was my birthday, and I thought it might be a hamper from Peggotty—but, alas! no; it was very sad news Mrs. Creakle had to give me—my dear mamma had died! Mrs. Creakle was very kind and gentle to me, and the boys, especially Traddles, were very sorry for me.

I went home the next day, and heard that the dear baby had died too. Peggotty received me with great tenderness, and told me about my mother's illness and how she had sent a loving message to me.

"Tell my dearest boy that his mother, as she lay here, blessed him not once, but a thousand times," and she had prayed to God to protect and keep her fatherless boy.

Mr. Murdstone did not take any notice of me, nor had Miss Murdstone a word of kindness for me. Peggotty was to leave in a month, and, to my great joy, I was allowed to go with her on a visit to Mr. Peggotty. On our way I found out that the mysterious message I had given to Peggotty meant that Barkis wanted to marry her, and Peggotty had consented. Everyone in Mr. Peggotty's cottage was pleased to see me, and did their best to comfort me. Little Em'ly was at school when I arrived, and I went out to meet her. I knew the way by which she would come, and presently found myself strolling along the path to meet her.

A figure appeared in the distance before long, and I soon knew it to be Em'ly, who was a little creature still in stature, though she was grown. But when she drew nearer, and I saw her blue eyes looking bluer, and her dimpled face looking brighter, and her own self prettier and gayer, a curious feeling came over me that made me pretend not to know her, and pass by as if I were looking at something a long way off. I have done such a thing since in later life, or I am mistaken.

Little Em'ly didn't care a bit. She saw me well enough; but instead of turning round and calling after me, ran away laughing. This obliged me to run after her, and she ran so fast that we were very near the cottage before I caught her.

"Oh, it's you, is it?" said little Em'ly.

"Why, you knew who it was, Em'ly," said I.

"And didn't *you* know who it was?" said Em'ly. I was going to kiss her, but she covered her cherry lips with her hands, and said she wasn't a baby now, and ran away, laughing more than ever, into the house.

She seemed to delight in teasing me, which was a change in her I wondered at very much. The tea-table was ready, and our little locker was put out in its old place, but instead of coming to sit by me, she went and bestowed her company upon that grumbling Mrs. Gummidge; and on Mr. Peggotty's inquiring why, rumpled her hair all over her face to hide it, and would do nothing but laugh.

"A little puss it is!" said Mr. Peggotty, patting her with his great white hand.

"Ah," said Mr. Peggotty, running his fingers through her bright curls, "here's another orphan, you see sir, and, here," giving Ham a back-handed knock in the chest, "is another of 'em, though he don't look much like it."

"If I had *you* for a guardian, Mr. Peggotty," said I, "I don't think I should *feel* much like it."

Em'ly was confused by our all observing her, and hung down her head, and her face was covered with blushes. Glancing up presently through her stray curls, and seeing that we were all looking at her still (I am sure I, for one, could have looked at her for hours), she ran away and kept away till it was nearly bedtime.

I lay down in the old little bed in the stern of the boat and the wind came moaning on across the flat as it had done before. But I could not help fancying now that it moaned of those who were gone; and instead of thinking that the sea might rise in the night and float the boat away, I thought of the sea that had risen, since I last heard those sounds, and drowned my happy home. I recollect, as the wind and water began to sound fainter in my ears, putting a short clause into my prayers, petitioning that I might grow up to marry little Em'ly, and so dropping lovingly asleep.

During this visit Peggotty was married to Mr. Barkis, and had a nice little house of her own, and I spent the night before I was to return home in a little room in the roof.

"Young or old, Davy dear, so long as I have this house over my head," said Peggotty, "you shall find it as if I expected you here directly every minute. I shall keep it as I used to keep your old little room, my darling, and if you was to go to China you might think of its being kept just the same all the time you were away."

I felt how good and true a friend she was, and thanked her as well as I could, for they had brought me to the gate of my home, and Peggotty had me clasped in her arms.

I was poor and lonely at home, with no one near to speak a loving word, or a face to look on with love or liking, only the two persons who had broken my mother's heart. How utterly wretched and forlorn I felt! I found I was not to go back to school any more, and wandered about sad and solitary, neglected and uncared for. Peggotty's weekly visits were my only comfort. I longed to go to school, however hard an one, to be taught something anyhow, anywhere— but no one took any pains with me, and I had no friends near who could help me.

At last one day, after some weary months had passed, Mr. Murdstone told me I was to go to London and earn my own living. There was a place for me at Murdstone & Grinby's, a firm in the wine trade. My lodging and clothes would be provided for me by my step-father, and I would earn enough for my food and pocket money. The next day I was sent up to London with the manager, dressed in a shabby little white hat with black crape round it for my mother, a black jacket, and hard, stiff corduroy trousers, a little fellow of ten years old, to fight my own battles with the world.

My place, I found, was one of the lowest in the firm of Murdstone & Grinby, with boys of no education and in quite an inferior station to myself—my duties were to wash the bottles, stick on labels, and so on. I was utterly miserable at being degraded in this way, when I thought of my former companions, Steerforth and Traddles, and my hopes of becoming a learned and distinguished man, and shed bitter tears, as I feared I would forget all I had learnt at school. My lodging, one bare little room, was in the house of some people named Micawber, shiftless, careless, good-natured people, who were always in debt and difficulties. I felt great pity for their misfortunes and did what I could to help poor Mrs. Micawber to sell her books and other little things she could spare, to buy food for herself, her husband, and their four children. I was too young and childish to know how to provide properly for myself, and often found I was obliged to live on bread and slices of cold pudding at the end of the week. If I had not been a very innocent-minded, good little boy, I might easily have fallen into bad ways at this time. But God took care of me and kept me from harm. I would not even tell Peggotty how miserable I was, for fear of distressing her.

The troubles of the Micawbers increased more and more, until at last they were obliged to leave London. I was very sad at this, for I had been with them so long that I felt they were my friends, and the prospect of being once more utterly alone, and having to find a lodging with strangers, made me so unhappy that I determined to endure this sort of life no longer. The last Sunday the Micawbers were in town I dined with them. I had bought a spotted horse for their little boy and a doll for the little girl, and had saved up a shilling for the poor servant-girl. After I had seen them off the next morning by the coach, I wrote to Peggotty to ask her if she knew where my aunt, Miss Betsy Trotwood, lived, and to borrow half-a-guinea; for I had resolved to run away from

Murdstone & Grinby's, and go to this aunt and tell her my
story. I remembered my mother telling me of her visit when
I was a baby, and that she fancied Miss Betsy had stroked
her hair gently, and this gave me courage to appeal to her.
Peggotty wrote, enclosing the half-guinea, and saying she
only knew Miss Trotwood lived near Dover, but whether in
that place itself or at Folkestone, Sandgate, or Hythe, she
could not tell. Hearing that all these places were close together, I made up my mind to start. As I had received my
week's wages in advance, I waited till the following Saturday, thinking it would not be honest to go before. I went
out to look for someone to carry my box to the coach office,
and unfortunately employed a wicked young man who not
only ran off with the box, but robbed me of my half-guinea,
leaving me in dire distress. In despair, I started off to walk
to Dover, and was forced to sell my waistcoat to buy some
bread. The first night I found my way to my old school at
Blackheath, and slept on a haystack close by, feeling some
comfort in the thought of the boys being near. I knew
Steerforth had left, or I would have tried to see him.

On I trudged the next day and sold my jacket at Chat-
ham to a dreadful old man, who kept me waiting all day for
the money, which was only one shilling and fourpence. I
was afraid to buy anything but bread or to spend any money
on a bed or a shelter for the night, and was terribly frightened by some rough tramps, who threw stones at me when I
did not answer to their calls. After six days, I arrived at
Dover, ragged, dusty and half-dead with hunger and fatigue.
But here, at first, I could get no tidings of my aunt, and, in
despair, was going to try some of the other places Peggotty
had mentioned, when the driver of a fly dropped his horse-
cloth, and as I was handing it up to him, I saw something

kind in the man's face that encouraged me to ask once more
if he knew where Miss Trotwood lived.

The man directed me towards some houses on the
heights, and thither I toiled.   Going into a little shop, I by
chance met with Miss Trotwood's maid, who showed me the
house, and went in leaving me standing at the gate, a forlorn
little creature, without a jacket or waistcoat, my white hat
crushed out of shape, my shoes worn out, my shirt and
trousers torn and stained, my pretty curly hair tangled, my
face and hands sunburnt and covered with dust. Lifting my
eyes to one of the windows above, I saw a pleasant-faced
gentleman with gray hair, who nodded at me several times,
then shook his head and went away.   I was just turning
away to think what I should do, when a tall, erect, eldery
lady, with a gardening apron on and a knife in her hand,
came out of the house, and began to dig up a root in the
garden.

"Go away," she said.   "Go away.   No boys here."

But I felt desperate.   Going in softly, I stood beside
her and touched her with my finger, and said, timidly, "If
you please, ma'am——" and when she looked up, I went
on—

"Please, aunt, I am your nephew!"

"Oh, Lord!" she exclaimed in astonishment, and sat
flat down on the path, staring at me, while I went on—

"I am David Copperfield, of Blunderstone, in Suffolk,
where you came the night I was born, and saw my dear
mamma.   I have been very unhappy since she died.   I have
been slighted and taught nothing, and thrown upon myself,
and put to work not fit for me.   It made me run away to
you.   I was robbed at first starting out and have walked all
the way, and have never slept in a bed since I began the

journey." Here I broke into a passion of crying, and my
aunt jumped up and took me into the house, where she
opened a cupboard and took out some bottles, pouring
some of the contents of each into my mouth, not noticing in
her agitation what they were, for I fancied I tasted anise-
seed water, anchovy sauce and salad dressing! Then she
put me on the sofa and sent the servant to ask "Mr. Dick"

"WELL, IF I WAS YOU I SHOULD WASH HIM," SAID MR. DICK.

put me on the sofa and sent the servant to ask "Mr. Dick"
to come down. The gentleman whom I had seen at the
window came in and was told by Miss Trotwood who the
ragged little object on the sofa was, and she finished by
saying—
13

"Now here you see young David Copperfield, and the question is what shall I do with him?"

"Do with him?" answered Mr. Dick. Then, after some consideration, and looking at me, he said, "Well, if I was you I should wash him!"

Miss Trotwood was quite pleased at this, and a warm bath was got ready at once, after which I was dressed in a shirt and trousers belonging to Mr. Dick (for Janet had burnt my rags), rolled up in several shawls, and put on the sofa till dinner-time, where I slept, and woke with the impression that my aunt had come and put my hair off my face, and murmured, "Pretty fellow, poor fellow."

After dinner I had to tell my story all over again to my aunt and Mr. Dick. Miss Trotwood again asked Mr. Dick's advice, and was delighted when that gentleman suggested I should be put to bed. I knelt down to say my prayers that night in a pleasant room facing the sea, and as I lay in the clean, snow-white bed I felt so grateful and comforted that I prayed earnestly I might never be homeless again, and might never forget the homeless.

The next morning my aunt told me she had written to Mr. Murdstone. I was alarmed to think that my step-father knew where I was, and exclaimed—

"Oh, I don't know what I shall do if I have to go back to Mr. Murdstone!"

But my aunt said nothing of her intentions, and I was uncertain what was to become of me. I hoped she might befriend me.

At last Mr. and Miss Murdstone arrived. To Miss Betsy's great indignation, Miss Murdstone rode a donkey across the green in front of the house, and stopped at the gate. Nothing made Miss Trotwood so angry as to see donkeys on that green, and I had already seen several battles between my aunt or Janet and the donkey boys.

After driving away the donkey and the boy who had dared to bring it there, Miss Trotwood received her visitors. She kept me near her, fenced in with a chair.

Mr. Murdstone told Miss Betsy that I was a very bad, stubborn, violent-tempered boy, whom he had tried to improve, but could not succeed; that he had put me in a respectable business from which I had run away. If Miss Trotwood chose to protect and encourage me now, she must do it always, for he had come to fetch me away there and then, and if I was not ready to come, and Miss Trotwood did not wish to give me up to be dealt with exactly as Mr. Murdstone liked, he would cast me off for always, and have no more to do with me.

"Are you ready to go, David?" asked my aunt.

But I answered no, and begged and prayed her for my father's sake to befriend and protect me, for neither Mr. nor Miss Murdstone had ever liked me or been kind to me and had made my mamma, who always loved me dearly, very unhappy about me, and I had been very miserable.

"Mr. Dick," said Miss Trotwood, "what shall I do with this child?"

Mr. Dick considered. "Have him measured for a suit of clothes directly."

"Mr. Dick," said Miss Trotwood, "your commonsense is invaluable."

Then she pulled me towards her, and said to Mr. Murdstone, "You can go when you like. I'll take my chance with the boy. If he's all you say he is I can at least do as much for him as you have done. But I don't believe a word of it."

Then she told Mr. Murdstone what she thought of the way he had treated me and my mother, which did not make that gentleman feel very comfortable, and finished by turning to Miss Murdstone and saying—

"Good-day to you, too, ma'am, and if I ever see you ride a donkey across my green again, as sure as you have a head upon your shoulders I'll knock your bonnet off and tread upon it!"

This startled Miss Murdstone so much that she went off quietly with her brother, while I, overjoyed, threw my arms round my aunt's neck, and kissed and thanked her with great heartiness.

Some clothes were bought for me that same day and marked "Trotwood Copperfield," for my aunt wished to call me by her name.

Now I felt my troubles were over, and I began quite a new life, well cared for and kindly treated. I was sent to a very nice school in Canterbury, where my aunt left me with these words, which I never forgot:

"Trot, be a credit to yourself, to me, and Mr. Dick, and heaven be with you. Never be mean in anything, never be false, never be cruel. Avoid these three vices, Trot, and I shall always be hopeful of you!"

I did my best to show my gratitude to my dear aunt by studying hard, and trying to be all she could wish.

When you are older you can read how Little David Copperfield grew up to be a good, clever man, and met again all his old friends, and made many new ones.

Also, what became of Steerforth, Traddles, the Peggottys, little Em'ly, and the Micawbers.

Jenny Wren.

WALKING into the city one holiday, a great many years ago, a gentleman ran up the steps of a tall house in the neighborhood of St. Mary Axe. The lower windows were those of a counting-house, but the blinds, like those of the entire front of the house, were drawn down.

The gentleman knocked and rang several times before anyone came, but at last an old man opened the door.

"What are you up to that you did not hear me?" said Mr. Fledgeby irritably.

"I was taking the air at the top of the house, sir," said the old man meekly, "it being a holiday. What might you please to want, sir?"

"Humph! Holiday indeed," grumbled his master, who was a toy merchant amongst other things. He then seated himself in the counting house and gave the old man—a Jew and Riah by name—directions about the dressing of some dolls about which he had come to speak, and, as he rose to go, exclaimed—

"By-the-by, how *do* you take the air? Do you stick your head out of a chimney-pot?"

"No, sir, I have made a little garden on the leads."

"Let's look at it," said Mr. Fledgeby.

"Sir, I have company there," returned Riah hesitating, "but will you please come up and see them?"

Mr. Fledgeby nodded, and, passing his master with a bow, the old man led the way up flight after flight of stairs, till they arrived at the housetop. Seated on a carpet, and

leaning against a chimney-stack, were two girls bending over
books. Some humble creepers were trained round the

"SEATED ON THE CARPET WERE TWO GIRLS.'

chimney-pots, and evergreens were placed round the roof,
and a few more books, a basket of gaily colored scraps, and
bits of tinsel, and another of common print stuff lay near.
One of the girls rose on seeing that Riah had brought a

visitor, but the other remarked, "I'm the person of the house downstairs, but I can't get up, whoever you are, because my back is bad and my legs are queer."

"This is my master," said Riah, speaking to the two girls, "and this," he added, turning to Mr. Fledgeby, "is Miss Jenny Wren; she lives in this house, and is a clever dressmaker for little people. Her friend Lizzie," continued Riah, introducing the second girl. "They are good girls, both, and as busy as they are good; in spare moments they come up here and take a book learning."

"We are glad to come up here for rest, sir," said Lizzie, with a grateful look at the old Jew. "No one can tell the rest that this place is to us."

"Humph!" said Mr. Fledgeby, looking round, "Humph!" He was so much surprised that apparently he couldn't get beyond that word, and as he went down again the old chimney-pots in their black cowls seemed to turn round and look after him as if they were saying "Humph" too.

Lizzie, the elder of these two girls, was strong and handsome, but little Jennie Wren, whom she so loved and protected, was small and deformed, though she had a beautiful little face, and the longest and loveliest golden hair in the world, which fell about her like a cloak of shining curls, as though to hide the poor little mis-shapen figure.

The Jew Riah, as well as Lizzie, was always kind and gentle to Jenny Wren, who called him her godfather. She had a father, who shared her poor little rooms, whom she called her child, for he was a bad, drunken, disreputable old man, and the poor girl had to care for him, and earn money to keep them both. She suffered a great deal, for the poor little bent back always ached sadly, and was often weary from incessant work, but it was only on rare occasions, when alone

or with her friend Lizzie, who often brought her work and
sat in Jenny's room, that the brave child ever complained of
her hard lot. Sometimes the two girls, Jenny helping herself along with a crutch, would go and walk about the
fashionable streets, in order to note how the grand folks

"GO ALONG WITH YOU, YOU WICKED OLD CHILD, I KNOW WHERE YOU HAVE BEEN!"

were dressed. As they walked along, Jennie would tell her
friend of the fancies she had when sitting alone at her work.
"I imagine birds till I can hear them sing," she said one
day, "and flowers till I can smell them. And oh! the
beautiful children that come to me in the early mornings!
They are quite different to other children, not like me, never
cold, or anxious, or tired, or hungry, never any pain; they
come in numbers, in long bright slanting rows, all dressed

JENNY WREN

in white, and with shiny heads. 'Who is this in pain?'
they say, and they sweep around and about me, take me up
in their arms, and I feel so light, and all the pain goes. I
know when they are coming a long way off, by hearing them
say, 'Who is this in pain?' and I answer, 'Oh my blessed
children, its poor me! have pity on me, and take me up and
then the pain will go.'"

Lizzie sat stroking and brushing the beautiful hair,
whilst the tired little dressmaker leant against her when they
were at home again, and as she kissed her good-night a
miserable old man stumbled into the room. "How's my
Jenny Wren, best of children?" he mumbled, as he shuffled
unsteadily towards her, but Jenny pointed her small finger
towards him, exclaiming—"Go along with you, you bad,
wicked old child, you troublesome, wicked old thing, *I* know
where you have been, *I* know your tricks and your manners."
The wretched man began to whimper, like a scolded child.
"Slave, slave, slave, from morning to night," went on
Jennie, still shaking her finger at him, "and all for this;
ain't you ashamed of yourself, you disgraceful boy?"

"Yes; my dear, yes," stammered the tipsy old father,
tumbling into a corner. Thus was the poor little dolls'
dressmaker dragged down day by day by the very hands
that should have cared for and held her up; poor, poor little
dolls' dressmaker! One day when Jenny was on her way
home with Riah, who had accompanied her on one of her
expeditions to the West End, they came on a small crowd
of people. A tipsy man had been knocked down and badly
hurt. "Let us see what it is," said Jenny, coming swiftly
forward on her crutches. The next moment she exclaimed
—"Oh, gentlemen—gentlemen, he is my child, he belongs
to me, my poor, bad old child!"

"Your child—belongs to you," repeated the man who was about to lift the helpless figure onto a stretcher, which had been brought for the purpose. "Aye, it's old Dolls—tipsy old Dolls," cried someone in the crowd, for it was by this name that they knew the old man.

"He's her father, sir," said Riah in a low tone to the doctor who was now bending over the stretcher.

"So much the worse," answered the doctor, "for the man is dead."

Yes, "Mr Dolls" was dead, and many were the dresses which the weary fingers of the sorrowful little worker must make in order to pay for his humble funeral and buy a black frock for herself. Riah sat by her in her poor room, saying a word of comfort now and then, and Lizzie came and went, and did all manner of little things to help her; but often the tears rolled down on to her work. "My poor child," she said to Riah, "my poor old child, and to think I scolded him so."

"You were always a good, brave, patient girl," returned Riah, smiling a little over her quaint fancy about her *child*, "always good and patient, however tired."

And so the poor little "person of the house" was left alone but for the faithful affection of the kind Jew and her friend Lizzie. Her room grew pretty and comfortable, for she was in great request in her "profession," as she called it, and there was now no one to spend and waste her earnings. But nothing could make her life otherwise than a suffering one till the happy morning when her child-angels visited her for the last time and carried her away to the land where all such pain as hers is healed for evermore.

Pip's Adventure.

"PIP, OLD CHAP, YOU'LL DO YOURSELF A MISCHIEF."

ALL that little Philip Pirrip, usually called Pip, knew about his father and mother, and his five little brothers, was from seeing their tombstones in the churchyard. He was taken care of by his sister, who was twenty years older than himself. She had married a blacksmith, named Joe Gargery, a kind, good man, while she, unfortunately, was a hard, stern woman, and treated her little brother and her amiable husband with great harshness. They lived in a marshy part of the country, about twenty miles from the sea.

One cold, raw day toward evening, when Pip was about six years old, he had wandered into the churchyard, and trying to make out what he could of the inscriptions on his family tombstones, and, the darkness coming on, he felt very lonely and frightened, and began to cry.

"Hold your noise!" cried a terrible voice, and a man started up from among the graves close to him. "Keep still, you little imp, or I'll cut your throat!"

He was a dreadful looking man, dressed in coarse gray cloth, with a great iron on his leg. Wet, muddy and miserable, he limped and shivered, and glared and growled; his teeth chattered in his head as he seized Pip by the chin.

"Oh! don't cut my throat, sir," cried Pip, in terror. "Pray don't do it, sir."

"Tell us your name!" said the man. "Quick!"

"Pip, sir."

"Once more," said the man staring at him. "Give it mouth."

"Pip, sir."

"Show us where you live," said the man. "Point out the place."

Pip showed him the village, about a mile or more from the church.

The man looked at him for a moment, and then turned him upside down and emptied his pockets. He found nothing in them but a piece of bread, which he ate ravenously.

"You young dog," said the man, licking his lips, "what fat cheeks you ha'e got . . . Darn me if I couldn't eat 'em, and if I han't half a mind to!"

Pip said earnestly that he hoped he would not.

"Now lookee here," said the man. "Where's your mother?"

"There, sir," said Pip.

At this the man started and seemed about to run away, but stopped and looked over his shoulder.

"There sir," explained Pip, showing him the tombstone.

"Oh, and is that your father along of your mother?"

"Yes sir," said Pip.

"Ha!" muttered the man, "then who d'ye live with?—supposin' you're kindly let to live, which I han't made up my mind about."

"My sister, sir, Mrs. Joe Gargery, wife of Joe Gargery, the blacksmith, sir."

"Blacksmith, eh?" said the man, and looked down at his leg. Then he seized the trembling little boy by both arms, and glaring down at him he said—

"Now lookee here, the question being whether you're to be let to live. You know what a file is?"

"Yes sir."

"And you know what wittles is?"

"Yes sir."

"You get me a file, and you get me wittles—you bring 'em both to me." All this time he was tilting poor Pip backwards till he was so dreadfully frightened and giddy that he clung to the man with both hands.

"You bring me, to-morrow morning early, that file and them wittles. You do it, and you never dare to say a word or dare to make a sign concerning your having seen such a person as me, or any person sumever, and you shall be let to live." Then he threatened all sorts of dreadful and terrible things to poor Pip if he failed to do all he had commanded, and made him solemnly promise to bring him what he wanted, and to keep the secret.   Then he let him go, saying, "You remember what you've undertook, and you get home."

"Goo—good night, sir," faltered Pip.

"Much of that!" said he glancing over the cold wet flat. "I wish I was a frog or a eel!"

Pip ran home without stopping.   Joe was sitting in the chimney corner, and told him Mrs. Joe had been out to look for him, and taken Tickler with her.   Tickler was a cane, and Pip was rather depressed by this piece of news.

Mrs. Joe came in almost directly, and, after having given Pip a taste of Tickler, she sat down to prepare the tea, and, cutting a huge slice of bread and butter, she gave half of it to Joe and half to Pip.   Pip managed, after some time, to slip his down the leg of his trousers, and Joe, thinking he had swallowed it, was dreadfully alarmed and begged him not to bolt his food like that.   "Pip, old chap, you'll do yourself a mischief—it'll stick somewhere, you can't have chewed it, Pip.   You know, Pip, you and me is always friends, and I'd be the last to tell upon you any time, but such a—such a most uncommon bolt as that." ·

"Been bolting his food, has he?" cried Mrs. Joe.

"You know, old chap," said Joe, "I bolted myself when I was your age—frequent—and as a boy I've been among a many bolters; but I never see your bolting equal yet, Pip, and it's a mercy you ain't bolted dead."

Mrs. Joe made a dive at Pip, fished him up by the hair, saying, "You come along and be dosed."

It was Christmas eve, and Pip had to stir the pudding from seven to eight, and found the bread and butter dreadfully in his way.   At last he slipped out and put it away in his little bedroom.

PIP AND THE
CONVICT.

Poor Pip passed a wretched night, thinking of the dreadful promise he had made, and as soon as it was begin-ning to get light outside he got up and crept downstairs, fancying that every board creaked out "Stop thief!" and "Get up, Mrs. Joe!"

As quickly as he could, he took some bread, some rind of cheese, about half a jar of mince-meat, which he tied up in a handkerchief, with the slice of bread and butter; some brandy from a stone bottle, a meat-bone with very little on it, and a pork-pie, which he found on an upper shelf. Then he got a file from among Joe's tools and ran for the marshes.

It was a very misty morning, and Pip imagined that all the cattle stared at him, as if to say, "Halloa, young thief!" and one black ox with a white cravat on, that made Pip think of a clergyman, looked so accusingly at him that Pip blubbered out, "I couldn't help it, sir! It wasn't for myself I took it."

Upon which the ox put down his head, blew a cloud of smoke out of his nose, and vanished with a kick-up of his hind legs, and a flourish of his tail.

Pip was soon at the Battery after that, and there was the man—hugging himself and limping to and fro, as if he had never all night left off hugging and limping. He was awfully cold, to be sure. Pip half expected to see him drop down before his face and die of cold. His eyes looked so aw-fully hungry, too, that when Pip handed him the file it occurred to him he would have tried to eat it, if he had not seen the bundle. He did not turn Pip upside down, this time, to get at what he had, but left him right side upward while he opened the bundle and emptied his pockets.

"What's in the bottle, boy?" said he.

"Brandy," said Pip.

He was already handing mince-pie down his throat in the most curious manner, more like a man who was putting it away somewhere in a violent hurry than a man who was eating it—but he left off to take some of the liquor, shivering all the while so violently that it was quite as much as he could do to keep the neck of the bottle between his teeth.

"I think you have got the ague," said Pip.

"I'm much of your opinion, boy," said he.

"It's bad about here. You've been lying out on the marshes, and they're dreadful aguish. Rheumatic, too."

"I'll eat my breakfast before they're the death of me," said he. "I'd do that, if I was going to be strung up to that there gallows as there is over there directly arterward. I'll beat the shivers so far, I'll bet you a guinea."

He was gobbling mince-meat, meat-bone, bread, cheese, and pork-pie all at once, staring distrustfully while he did so at the mist all round, and often stopping—even stopping his jaws—to listen. Some real or fancied sound, some clink upon the river or breathing of beasts upon the marsh, now gave him a start, and he said, suddenly:

"You're not a false imp? You brought no one with you?"

"No, sir! No!"

"Nor give no one the office to follow you?"

"No!"

"Well," said he, "I believe you. You'd be but a fierce young hound indeed, if at your time of life you should help to hunt a wretched warmint, hunted as near death and dunghill as this poor wretched warmint is!"

Something clicked in his throat, as if he had works in him like a clock, and was going to strike. And he smeared his ragged, rough sleeve over his eyes.

14

Pitying his desolation, and watching him as he gradu ally settled down upon the pie, Pip made bold to say, "I am glad you enjoy it."

"Did you speak?"

"I said I was glad you enjoyed it."

"Thankee, my boy. I do."

Pip had often watched a large dog eating his food; and he now noticed a decided similarity between the dog's way of eating and the man's. The man took strong, sharp, sudden bites, just like the dog. He swallowed, or rather snapped up, every mouthful too soon and too fast; and he looked sideways here and there while he ate, as if he thought there was danger of somebody's coming to take the pie away. He was altogether too unsettled in his mind over it to appreciate it comfortably, Pip thought, or to have anybody to dine with him, without making a chop with his jaws at the visitor. In all of which particulars he was very like the dog.

Pip watched him trying to file the iron off his leg, and then, being afraid of stopping longer away from home, he ran off.

Pip passed a wretched morning, expecting every moment that the disappearance of the pie would be found out. But Mrs. Joe was too much taken up with preparing the dinner, for they were expecting visitors, and were to have a superb dinner, consisting of a leg of pickled pork and greens, and a pair of roast stuffed fowls, a mince-pie, and a pudding.

Just at the end of the dinner Pip thought his time had come to be found out, for his sister said graciously to her guests—

"You must taste a most delightful and delicious present I have had. It's a pie, a savory pork-pie."

Pip could bear it no longer, and ran for the door, and there ran head foremost into a party of soldiers with their muskets, one of whom held out a pair of handcuffs to him, saying, "Here you are, look sharp, come on." But they had not come for him; they only wanted Joe to mend the handcuffs, for they were on the search for two convicts who had escaped and were somewhere hid in the marshes. This turned the attention of Mrs. Joe from the disappearance of the pie, without which she had come back, in great astonishment. When the handcuffs were mended the soldiers went off, accompanied by Joe and one of the visitors, and Joe took Pip and carried him on his back.

Pip whispered, "I hope, Joe, we shan't find them," and Joe answered, "I'd give a shilling if they had cut and run, Pip,"

But the soldiers soon caught them, and one was Pip's miserable acquaintance, and once, when the man looked at Pip, the child shook his head to try and let him know he had said nothing.

But the convict, without looking at anyone, told the sergeant he wanted to say something to prevent other people being under suspicion, and said he had taken some "wittles" from the blacksmith's. "It was some broken wittles, that's what it was, and a dram of liquor, and a pie."

"Have you happened to miss such an article as a pie, blacksmith?" inquired the sergeant.

"My wife did, at the very moment when you came in. Don't you know, Pip?"

"So," said the convict, looking at Joe, "you're the blacksmith, are you? Then, I'm sorry to say I've eat your pie."

"God knows you're welcome to it," said Joe. "We don't know what you have done, but we wouldn't have you starved to death for it, poor, miserable fellow-creature. Would us, Pip?"

Then the boat came, and the convicts were taken back to their prison, and Joe carried Pip home.

*   *   *   *   *   *   *

Some years after, some mysterious friend sent money for Pip to be educated and brought up as a gentleman, but it was only when Pip was quite grown up that he discovered this mysterious friend was the wretched convict who had frightened him so dreadfully that cold, dark Christmas eve.

The Child who Swallowed a Necklace.

"BY-THE-BY, Bob," said Hopkins, with a scarcely perceptible glance at Mr. Pickwick's attentive face, "we had a curious accident last night. A child was brought in who had swallowed a necklace."

"Swallowed what, sir?" interrupted Mr. Pickwick.

"A necklace," replied Jack Hopkins.

"Not all at once—you know that would be too much; *you* couldn't swallow that, if the child did—eh? Mr. Pickwick, ha! ha!" Mr. Hopkins appeared highly gratified with his own pleasantry, and continued: "No, the way was this: child's parents were poor people, who lived in a court. Child's eldest sister bought a necklace—common necklace, made of large, black, wooden beads. Child, being fond of toys, cribbed the necklace, hid it, played with it, cut the string, and swallowed a bead. Child thought it capital fun, went back next day and swallowed another bead."

"Bless my heart," said Mr. Pickwick, "what a dreadful thing! I beg your pardon, sir. Go on."

"Next day child swallowed two beads; the day after that he treated himself to three, and so on, till, in a week's time, he had got through the necklace, five-and-twenty beads in all. The sister, who was an industrious girl, and seldom treated herself to a bit of finery, cried her eyes out at the loss of the necklace; looked high and low for it; but I needn't say didn't find it. A few days afterwards the family were at dinner—baked shoulder of mutton, and potatoes under it—the child, who wasn't hungry, was playing about the room, when suddenly there was heard a singular noise, like a small hail-storm. 'Don't do that, my boy,' said the father. 'I ain't a-doin' nothin',' said the child. 'Well, don't do it again' said the father. There was a short silence, and then the noise began again, worse than ever. 'If you don't mind what I say, my boy,' said the father, 'you'll find yourself in bed, in something less than a pig's whisper.' He gave the child a shake to make him obedient, and such a rattling ensued as nobody ever heard before. 'Why it's *in* the child!' said the father; 'he's got the croup in the wrong place!' 'No I haven't, father,' said the child, beginning to cry, 'it's the necklace; I swallowed it, father.' The father caught the child up, and ran with him to the hospital—the beads in the boy's stomach rattling all the way with the jolting; and the people looking up in the air and down into the cellars, to see where the unusual sound came from. He's in the hospital now, and he makes such a strange noise when he walks about that they're obliged to muffle him in a watchman's coat, for fear he should wake the patients!"

"That's the most extraordinary case I ever heard of," said Mr. Pickwick, with an emphatic blow on the table.

Todgers'.

MR. PECKSNIFF with his two beautiful young daughters looked about him for a moment, and then knocked at the door of a very dingy edifice, even among the choice collection of dingy edifices at hand, on the front of which was a little oval board, like a tea-tray, with this inscription—"Commercial Boarding-house. M. Todgers."

It seemed that M. Todgers was not up yet, for Mr. Pecksniff knocked twice and rang thrice, without making any impression on anything but a dog over the way. At last a chain and some bolts were withdrawn with a rusty noise, and a small boy with a large red head, and no nose to speak of, and a very dirty boot on his left arm, appeared, who (being surprised) rubbed the nose just mentioned with the back of a shoe-brush, and said nothing.

"Still abed, my man?" asked Mr. Pecksniff.

"I WISH THEY WOS STILL ABED."

"Still abed!" replied the boy. "I wish they wos still abed. They're very noisy abed; all calling for their boots at once. I thought you was the Paper, and wondered why you didn't shove yourself through the grating as usual. What do you want?''

Considering his years, which were tender, the youth may be said to have asked this question sternly, and in something of a defiant manner. But Mr. Pecksniff, without taking um-brage at his bearing, put a card in his hand, and bade him take that upstairs, and show them in the meanwhile into a room where there was a fire.

Surely there never was, in any other borough, city, or hamlet in the world, such a singular sort of a place as Todgers'. And surely London, to judge from that part of it which hemmed Todgers' round, and hustled it and crushed it and stuck its brick and mortar elbows into it, and kept the air from it, and stood perpetually between it and the light, was worthy of Todgers'.

There were more trucks near Todgers' than you would suppose a whole city could ever need; not active trucks, but a vagabond race, forever lounging in the narrow lanes before their masters' doors and stopping up the pass; so that when a stray hackney-coach or lumbering wagon came that way they were the cause of such an uproar as enlivened the whole neighborhood, and made the very bells in the next church-tower vibrate again. In the throats and maws of dark nothorough-fares near Todgers', individual wine-merchants and whole-sale dealers in grocery-ware had perfect little towns of their own; and deep among the very foundations of these build-ings the ground was undermined and burrowed out into stables, where cart-horses, troubled by rats, might be heard on a quiet Sunday rattling their halters, as disturbed spirits in tales of haunted houses are said to clank their chains.

To tell of half the queer old taverns that had a drowsy and secret existence near Todgers' would fill a goodly book;

while a second volume, no less capacious, might be devoted
to an account of the quaint old guests who frequented their
dimly-lighted parlors.

The top of the house was worthy of notice. There was
a sort of terrace on the roof, with posts and fragments of rotten lines, once intended to dry clothes upon; and there were
two or three tea-chests out there, full of earth, with forgotten
plants in them, like old walking sticks. Whoever climbed
to this observatory was stunned at first from having
knocked his head against the little door in coming out; and,
after that, was for the moment choked from having looked,
perforce, straight down the kitchen chimney; but, these two
stages over, there were things to gaze at from the top of Todgers', well worth your seeing, too. For, first and foremost, if
the day were bright, you observed upon the house-tops, stretching far away, a long dark path—the shadow of the
Monument; and turning round, the tall original was close
beside you, with every hair erect upon his golden head, as if
the doings of the city frightened him. Then there were
steeples, towers, belfries, shining vanes and masts of ships,
a very forest. Gables, house-tops, garret-windows, wilderness upon wilderness. Smoke and noise enough for all the
world at once.

After the first glance, there were slight features in the
midst of this crowd of objects, which sprung out from the
mass without any reason, as it were, and took hold of the
attention whether the spectator would or no. Thus the re-
volving chimney-pots on one great stack of buildings seemed
to be turning gravely to each other every now and then, and
whispering the result of their separate observation of what
was going on below. Others, of a crook-backed shape,
appeared to be maliciously holding themselves askew, that

they might shut the prospect out and baffle Todgers. The man who was mending a pen at an upper window over the way became of paramount importance in the scene, and made a blank in it, ridiculously disproportionate in its extent, when he retired. The gambols of a piece of cloth upon the dyer's pole had far more interest for the moment than all the changing motion of the crowd. Yet even while the looker-on felt angry with himself for this, and wondered how it was, the tumult swelled into a roar; the hosts of objects seemed to thicken and expand a hundred fold; and after gazing round him, quite scared, he turned into Todgers' again, much more rapidly than he came out; and ten to one he told M. Todgers afterwards that if he hadn't done so he would certainly have come into the street by the shortest cut; that is to say, head-foremost.

So said the two Miss Pecksniffs, when they retired with Mrs. Todgers from this place of espial, leaving the youthful porter to close the door and follow them downstairs; who being of a playful temperament, and contemplating with a delight peculiar to his sex and time of life any chance of dashing himself into small fragments, lingered behind to walk upon the parapet.

It was the second day of their stay in London, and by this time the Miss Pecksniffs and Mrs. Todgers were becoming highly confidential, insomuch that the last-named lady had already communicated the particulars of three early disappointments of a tender nature, and had furthermore possessed her young friends with a general summary of the life, conduct and character of Mr. Todgers, who, it seemed, had cut his matrimonial career rather short, by unlawfully running away from his happiness, and establishing himself in foreign countries as a bachelor.

"Your pa was once a little particular in his attentions, my dears," said Mrs. Todgers, "but to be your ma was too much happiness denied me. You'd hardly know who this was done for, perhaps?"

She called their attention to an oval miniature, like a little blister, which was tacked up over the kettle-holder, and in which there was a dreamy shadowing forth of her own visage.

"It's a speaking likeness!" cried the two Miss Pecksniffs.

"It was considered so once," said Mrs. Todgers, warming herself in a gentlemanly manner at the fire: "but I hardly thought you would have known it, my loves."

They would have known it anywhere. If they could have met with it in the street or seen it in a shop-window they would have cried, "Good gracious! Mrs. Todgers!"

"Presiding over an establishment like this makes sad havoc with the features, my dear Miss Pecksniffs," said Mrs. Todgers. "The gravy alone is enough to add twenty years to one's age, I do assure you."

"Lor!" cried the two Miss Pecksniffs.

"The anxiety of that one item, my dears," said Mrs. Todgers, "keeps the mind continually upon the stretch. There is no such passion in human nature as the passion for gravy among commercial gentlemen. It's nothing to say a joint won't yield—a whole animal wouldn't yield— the amount of gravy they expect each day at dinner. And what I have undergone in consequence," cried Mrs. Todgers, raising her eyes and shaking her head, "no one would believe!"

"Just like Mr. Pinch, Mercy!" said Charity. "We have always noticed it in him, you remember?"

"Yes, my dear," giggled Mercy, "but we have never given it to him, you know."

"You, my dears, having to deal with your pa's pupils who can't help themselves, are able to take your own way," said Mrs. Todgers, "but in a commercial establishment, where any gentleman may say, any Saturday evening, 'Mrs. Todgers, this day week we part, in consequence of the cheese,' it is not so easy to preserve a pleasant understanding. Your pa was kind enough," added the good lady, "to invite me to take a ride with you to-day; and I think he mentioned that you were going to call upon Miss Pinch. Any relation to the gentleman you were speaking of just now, Miss Pecksniff?"

"For goodness' sake, Mrs. Todgers," interposed the lively Mercy, "don't call him a gentleman. My dear Cherry, Pinch a gentleman? The idea!"

"What a wicked girl you are!" cried Mrs. Todgers, embracing her with great affection. "You are quite a quiz, I do declare! My dear Miss Pecksniff, what a happiness your sister's spirits must be to your pa and self!"

"He's the most hideous, goggle-eyed creature, Mrs. Todgers, in existence," resumed Mercy; "quite an ogre. The ugliest, awkwardest, frightfullest being you can imagine. This is his sister, so I leave you to suppose what *she* is. I shall be obliged to laugh outright, I know I shall!" cried the charming girl. "I never shall be able to keep my countenance. The notion of a Miss Pinch presuming to exist at all is sufficient to kill one, but to see her—oh my stars!"

Mrs. Todgers laughed immensely at the dear love's humor, and declared she was quite afraid of her, that she was. She was so very severe.

"Who is severe?" cried a voice at the door. " There

is no such thing as severity in our family, I hope!" And then Mr. Pecksniff peeped smilingly into the room, and said, "May I come in, Mrs. Todgers?"

Mrs. Todgers almost screamed, for the little door of communication between that room and the inner one being wide open, there was a full disclosure of the sofa-bedstead in all its monstrous impropriety. But she had the presence of mind to close this portal in the twinkling of an eye; and having done so, said, though not without confusion, "Oh yes, Mr. Pecksniff, you can come in if you please."

"How are we to-day," said Mr. Pecksniff, jocosely; "and what are our plans? Are we ready to go and see Tom Pinch's sister? Ha, ha, ha! Poor Thomas Pinch!"

"Are we ready," returned Mrs. Todgers, nodding her head with mysterious intelligence, "to send a favorable reply to Mr. Jinkins' round-robin? That's the first question, Mr. Pecksniff."

"Why Mr. Jinkins' robin, my dear madam?" asked Mr. Pecksniff, putting one arm round Mercy and the other round Mrs. Todgers, whom he seemed, in the abstraction of the moment, to mistake for Charity. "Why Mr. Jinkins'?"

"Because he began to get it up, and indeed always takes the lead in the house," said Mrs. Todgers, playfully. "That's why, sir."

"Jinkins is a man of superior talents," observed Mr. Pecksniff. "I have conceived a great regard for Jinkins. I take Jinkins' desire to pay polite attention to my daughters as an additional proof of the friendly feelings of Jinkins, Mrs. Todgers."

"Well now," returned the lady, "having said so much, you must say the rest, Mr. Pecksniff; so tell the dear young ladies all about it."

With these words she gently eluded Mr. Pecksniff's grasp, and took Miss Charity into her own embrace; though whether she was impelled to this proceeding solely by the irrepressible affection she had conceived for that young lady, or whether it had any reference to a lowering, not to say distinctly spiteful expression which had been visible in her face for some moments, has never been exactly ascertained. Be this as it may, Mr. Pecksniff went on to inform his daughters of the purport and history of the round-robin aforesaid, which was, in brief, that the commercial gentleman who helped to make up the sum and substance of that noun of multitude signifying many, called Todgers, desired the honor of their presence at the general table so long as they remained in the house, and besought that they would grace the board at dinner-time next day, the same being Sunday. He further said that, Mrs. Todgers being a consenting party to this invitation, he was willing, for his part, to accept it; and so left them that he might write his gracious answer, the while they armed themselves with their best bonnets for the utter defeat and overthrow of Miss Pinch.

Tom Pinch's sister was governess in a family, a lofty family; perhaps the wealthiest brass and copper founder's family known to mankind. They lived at Camberwell; in a house so big and fierce that its mere outside, like the outside of a giant's castle, struck terror into vulgar minds and made bold persons quail. There was a great front gate, with a great bell, whose handle was in itself a note of admiration; and a great lodge, which, being close to the house, rather spoiled the look-out certainly, but made the look-in tremendous. At this entry a great porter kept constant watch and ward; and when he gave the visitor high leave to pass he rang a second great bell, responsive to whose note a great

footman appeared in due time at the great hall-door with
such great tags upon his liveried shoulders that he was perpetually entangling and hooking himself among the chairs
and tables and led a life of torment which could scarcely have
been surpassed if he had been a blue-bottle in a world of
cobwebs.

To this mansion Mr. Pecksniff, accompanied by his
daughters and Mrs. Todgers, drove gallantly in a one-horse
fly. The foregoing ceremonies having been all performed,
they were ushered into the house, and so, by degrees,
they got at last into a small room with books in it, where
Mr. Pinch's sister was at that moment instructing her eldest
pupil: to wit, a premature little woman thirteen years old,
who had already arrived at such a pitch of whalebone and
education that she had nothing girlish about her; which was
a source of great rejoicing to all her relations and friends.

"Visitors for Miss Pinch!" said the footman. He
must have been an ingenious young man, for he said it very
cleverly; with a nice discrimination between the cold respect
with which he would have announced visitors to the family
and the warm personal interest with which he would have
announced visitors to the cook.

"Visitors for Miss Pinch!"

Miss Pinch rose hastily with such tokens of agitation
as plainly declared that her list of callers was not numerous.
At the same time the little pupil became alarmingly upright, and prepared herself to take mental notes of all that
might be said and done. For the lady of the establishment was
curious in the natural history and habits of the animal called
Governess, and encouraged her daughters to report thereon
whenever occasion served; which was, in reference to all
parties concerned, very laudable, improving, and pleasant.

It is a melancholy fact, but it must be related, that Mr.
Pinch's sister was not at all ugly.   On the contrary, she had
a good face—a very mild and prepossessing face; and a
pretty little figure—slight and short, but remarkable for its
neatness.   There was something of her brother, much of
him indeed, in a certain gentleness of manner, and in her
look of timid trustfulness; but she was so far from being a
fright, or a dowdy, or a horror, or anything else predicted by
the two Miss Pecksniffs, that those young ladies naturally
regarded her with great indignation, feeling that this was by
no means what they had come to see.

Miss Mercy, as having the larger share of gayety, bore
up the best against this disappointment, and carried it off,
in outward show at least, with a titter; but her sister, not
caring to hide her disdain, expressed it pretty openly in her
looks.   As to Mrs. Todgers, she leaned on Mr. Pecksniff's
arm and preserved a kind of genteel grimness, suitable to
any state of mind, and involving any shade of opinion.

"Don't be alarmed, Miss Pinch," said Mr. Pecksniff,
taking her hand condescendingly in one of his, and patting
it with the other.   "I have called to see you, in pursuance
of a promise given to your brother, Thomas Pinch.   My
name—compose yourself, Miss Pinch—is Pecksniff."

The good man emphasized these words as though he
would have said, "You see in me, young person, the bene
factor of your race; the patron of your house; the preserver
of your brother, who is fed with manna daily from my table;
and in right of whom there is a considerable balance in my
favor at present standing in the books beyond the sky.   But
I have no pride, for I can afford to do without it!"

The poor girl felt it all as if it had been Gospel Truth.
Her brother, writing in the fullness of his simple heart, had

often told her so, and how much more! As Mr. Pecksniff ceased to speak, she hung her head, and dropped a tear upon his hand.

"Oh, very well, Miss Pinch!" thought the sharp pupil, "crying before strangers, as if you didn't like the situation!"

"Thomas is well," said Mr. Pecksniff; "and sends his love and this letter. I cannot say, poor fellow, that he will ever be distinguished in our profession; but he has the will to do well, which is the next thing to having the power, and, therefore, we must bear with him. Eh?"

"I know he has the will, sir," said Tom Pinch's sister, "and I know how kindly and considerately you cherish it, for which neither he nor I can ever be grateful enough, as we very often say in writing to each other. The young ladies too," she added, glancing gratefully at his two daughters. "I know how much we owe to them."

"My dears," said Mr. Pecksniff, turning to them with a smile; "Thomas' sister is saying something you will be glad to hear, I think."

"We can't take any merit to ourselves, papa!" cried Cherry, as they both apprised Tom Pinch's sister, with a courtesy, that they would feel obliged if she would keep her distance. "Mr. Pinch's being so well provided for is owing to you alone, and we can only say how glad we are to hear that he is as grateful as he ought to be."

"Oh, very well, Miss Pinch!" thought the pupil again. "Got a grateful brother, living on other people's kindness."

"It was very kind of you," said Tom Pinch's sister, with Tom's own simplicity and Tom's own smile, "to come here—very kind indeed; though how great a kindness you have done me in gratifying my wish to see you, and to thank

15

you with my own lips, you, who make so light of benefits conferred, can scarcely think."

"Very grateful; very pleasant; very proper," murmured Mr. Pecksniff.

"It makes me happy, too," said Ruth Pinch, who, now that her first surprise was over, had a chatty, cheerful way with her, and a single-hearted desire to look upon the best side of everything, which was the very moral and image of Tom; "very happy to think that you will be able to tell him how more than comfortably I am situated here, and how unnecessary it is that he should ever waste a regret on my being cast upon my own resources. Dear me! So long as I heard that he was happy and he heard that I was," said Tom's sister, "we could both bear, without one impatient or complaining thought, a great deal more than ever we have had to endure, I am very certain." And if ever the plain truth were spoken on this occasionally false earth, Tom's sister spoke it when she said that.

"Ah!" cried Mr. Pecksniff, whose eyes had in the meantime wandered to the pupil; "certainly. And how do *you* do, my very interesting child?"

"Quite well, I thank you, sir," replied that frosty innocent.

"A sweet face this, my dears," said Mr. Pecksniff, turning to his daughters. "A charming manner!"

Both young ladies had been in ecstasies with the scion of a wealthy house (through whom the nearest road and shortest cut to her parents might be supposed to lie) from the first. Mrs. Todgers vowed that anything one-quarter so angelic she had never seen. "She wanted but a pair of wings, a dear," said that good woman, "to be a young syrup," meaning, possibly, young sylph or seraph.

"If you will give that to your distinguished parents, my amiable little friend," said Mr. Pecksniff, producing one of his professional cards, "and will say that I and my daughters——"

"And Mrs. Todgers, pa," said Mercy.

"I SAY—THERE'S FOWLS TO-MORROW. NOT SKINNY ONES. OH NO!"

"And Mrs. Todgers, of London," added Mr. Pecksniff, "that I, and my daughters, and Mrs. Todgers, of London, did not intrude upon them, as our object simply was to take some notice of Miss Pinch, whose brother is a young man in my employment; but that I could not leave this very chaste mansion without adding my humble tribute, as an architect, to the correctness and elegence of the owner's taste, and to his just appreciation of that beautiful art, to the cultivation of which I have devoted a life, and to the promotion of whose glory and advancement I have sacrificed a—a fortune—I shall be very much obliged to you."

"Missis' compliments to Miss Pinch," said the footman, suddenly appearing, and speaking in exactly the same key as before, "and begs to know wot my young lady is a-learning of just now."

"Oh!" said Mr, Pecksniff, "here is the young man. *He* will take the card. With my compliments, if you please, young man. My dears, we are interrupting the studies. Let us go."

One evening, following the visit to Miss Pinch, there was a great bustle at Todgers', partly owing to some additional domestic preparations for the morrow and partly to the excitement always inseparable in that house from Saturday night, when every gentleman's linen arrived at a different hour in his own little bundle, with his private account pinned on the outside. Shrill altercations from time to time arose between Mrs. Todgers and the girl in remote back kitchens; and sounds were occasionally heard, indicative of small articles of iron-mongery and hardware being thrown at the boy. It was the custom of that youth on Saturdays to roll up his shirt sleeves to his shoulders, and pervade all parts of the house in an apron of coarse green baize; moreover, he was more strongly tempted on Saturdays than any other days (it being a busy time) to make bolts into the neighboring alleys when he answered the door, and there to play at leap-frog and other sports with vagrant lads, until pursued and brought back by the hair of his head or the lobe of his ear; thus, he was quite a conspicuous feature among the peculiar incidents of the last day in the week at Todgers'.

He was especially so on this particular Saturday evening and honored the Miss Pecksniffs with a deal of notice; seldom passing the door of Mrs. Todgers' private room, where they sat alone before the fire, without putting in his head and greeting them with some such compliments as, "There you are agin!" "Ain't it nice?"—and similar humorous attentions.

"I say," he whispered, stopping in one of his journeys to and fro, "young ladies, there's soup to-morrow. She's a-making it now. Ain't she a-putting in the water! Oh! not at all, neither!"

In the course of answering another knock he thrust in his head again.

"I say—there's fowls to-morrow. Not skinny ones. Oh no!"

Presently he called through the keyhole:

"There's a fish to-morrow—just come. Don't eat none of him!" and with this spectral warning, vanished again.

By-and-by he returned to lay the cloth for supper. He entertained them on this occasion by thrusting the lighted candle into his mouth, and exhibiting his face in a state of transparency; after the performance of which feat he went on with his professional duties; brightening every knife as he laid it on the table, by breathing on the blade and afterwards polishing the same on the apron already mentioned. When he had completed his preparations he grinned at the sisters, and expressed his belief that the approaching collation would be of "rather a spicy sort."

"Will it be long before it's ready, Bailey?" asked Mercy.

"No," said Bailey, "it *is* cooked. When I come up

she was dodging among the tender pieces with a fork, and eating of 'em."

But he had scarcely achieved the utterance of these words when he received a manual compliment on the head which sent him staggering against the wall, and Mrs. Todgers, dish in hand, stood indignantly before him.

"Oh you little villain!" said that lady. "Oh you bad, false boy!"

"No worse than yerself," retorted Bailey, guarding his head, on a principle invented by Mr. Thomas Cribb. "Ah! Come now! Do that agin, will yer?"

"He's the most dreadful child," said Mrs. Todgers, setting down the dish, "I ever had to deal with. The gentlemen spoil him to that extent, and teach him such things, that I'm afraid nothing but hanging will ever do him any good."

"Won't it!" cried Bailey. "Oh! Yes! Wot do you go a-lowerin' the table-beer for, then, and destroying my constitooshun?"

"Go downstairs, you vicious boy!" said Mrs. Todgers, holding the door open. "Do you hear me? Go along!"

After two or three dexterous feints he went, and was seen no more that night, save once, when he brought up some tumblers and hot water, and much disturbed the two Miss Pecksniffs by squinting hideously behind the back of the unconscious Mrs. Todgers. Having done this justice to his wounded feelings, he retired under-ground; where, in company with a swarm of black beetles and a kitchen candle, he employed his faculties in cleaning boots and brushing clothes until the night was far advanced.

Benjamin was supposed to be the real name of this young retainer, but he was known by a great variety of names. Benjamin, for instance, had been converted into Uncle Ben, and that again had been corrupted into Uncle. The gentlemen at Todgers' had a merry habit, too, of bestowing upon him, for the time being, the name of any notorious malefactor or minister, and sometimes, when current events were flat, they even sought the pages of history for these distinctions; as Mr. Pitt, Young Brownrigg, and the like. At the period of which we write he was generally known among the gentlemen as Bailey junior, a name bestowed upon him in contradistinction, perhaps, to Old Bailey; and possibly as involving the recollection of an unfortunate lady of the same name, who perished by her own hand early in life, and has been immortalized in a ballad.

The usual Sunday dinner-hour at Todgers' was two o'clock—a suitable time, it was considered, for all parties; convenient to Mrs. Todgers, on account of the bakers; and convenient to the gentlemen, with reference to their afternoon engagements. But on the Sunday which was to introduce the two Miss Pecksniffs to a full knowledge of Todgers' and its society, the dinner was postponed until five, in order that everything might be as genteel as the occasion demanded.

When the hour drew nigh, Bailey junior, testifying great excitement, appeared in a complete suit of cast-off clothes several sizes too large for him, and, in particular, mounted a clean shirt of such extraordinary magnitude that one of the gentlemen (remarkable for his ready wit) called him "collars" on the spot. At about a quarter before five a deputation, consisting of Mr. Jinkins and another gentleman whose name was Gander, knocked at the door of Mrs. Todgers' room, and, being formally introduced to the two Miss Pecksniffs by their parent, who was in waiting, besought the honor of conducting them upstairs.

Here the gentlemen were all assembled.　There was a general cry of "Hear, hear!" and "Bravo, Jink!" when Mr. Jinkins appeared with Charity on his arm; which became quite rapturous as Mr. Gander followed, escorting Mercy, and Mr. Pecksniff brought up the rear with Mrs. Todgers.

"The wittles is up!"

Dick Swiveller and the Marchioness.

RICHARD SWIVELLER, a good-hearted, t h o u g h somewhat erratic young man, the clerk of Sampson Brass, a scheming lawyer, often found time hanging heavily on his hands, and for the better preservation of his cheerfulness therefore, and to prevent his faculties from rusting, he provided himself with a cribbage-board and pack of cards, and accustomed himself to play at cribbage with a dummy, for twenty, thirty, or sometimes even fifty thousand pounds a side, besides many hazardous bets to a considerable amount.

As these games were very silently conducted, notwithstanding the magnitude of the interests involved, Mr. Swiveller began to think that on those evenings when Mr. and Miss Brass were out (and they often went out now) he heard a kind of snorting or hard-breathing sound in the direction of the door, which it occurred to him, after some reflection, must proceed from the small servant, who always had a cold from damp living. Looking intently that way one night, he plainly distinguished an eye gleaming and glistening at the keyhole; and having now no doubt that his suspicions were correct, he stole softly to the door and pounced upon her before she was aware of his approach.

"Oh! I didn't mean any harm indeed. Upon my word I didn't," cried the small servant, struggling like a much larger one. "It's so very dull downstairs. Please don't you tell upon me; please don't."

"Tell upon you!" said Dick. "Do you mean to say you were looking through the keyhole for company?"

233

"Yes, upon my word I was," replied the small servant.

"How long have you been cooling your eye there," said Dick.

"Oh, ever since you first began to play them cards, and long before."

Vague recollections of several fantastic exercises with which he had refreshed himself after the fatigues of business, and to all of which, no doubt, the small servant was a party, rather disconcerted Mr. Swiveller; but he was not very sensitive on such points, and recovered himself speedily.

"Well—come in," he said, after a little consideration. "Here—sit down, and I'll teach you how to play."

"Oh! I durstn't do it," rejoined the small servant. "Miss Sally 'ud kill me if she know'd I came up here."

"Have you got a fire downstairs?" said Dick.

"A very little one," replied the small servant.

"Miss Sally couldn't kill me if she know'd I went down there, so I'll come," said Richard, putting the cards into his pocket. "Why, how thin you are! What do you mean by it?"

"It ain't my fault."

"Could you eat any bread and meat?" said Dick, taking down his hat. "Yes? Ah! I thought so. Did you ever taste beer?"

"I had a sip of it once," said the small servant.

"Here's a state of things!" cried Mr. Swiveller, raising his eyes to the ceiling. "She *never* tasted it—it can't be tasted in a sip! Why, how old are you?"

"I don't know."

Mr. Swiveller opened his eyes very wide and appeared thoughtful for a moment; then, bidding the child mind the door until he came back, vanished straightway.

Presently he returned, followed by the boy from the public house, who bore in one hand a plate of bread and beef and in the other a great pot, filled with some very fragrant compound, which sent forth a grateful steam, and was indeed choice purl, made after a particular receipt which Mr. Swiveller had imparted to the landlord at a period when he was deep in his books and desirous to conciliate his friendship. Relieving the boy of his burden at the door, and charging his little companion to fasten it to prevent surprise, Mr. Swiveller followed her into the kitchen. "There!" said Richard, putting the plate before her. "First of all, clear that off, and then you'll see what's next."

The small servant needed no second bidding, and the plate was soon empty.

"Next," said Dick, handing the purl, "take a pull at that; but moderate your transports, you know, for you're not used to it. Well, is it good?"

"Oh! isn't it?" said the small servant.

Mr. Swiveller appeared gratified beyond all expression by this reply, and took a long draught himself, steadfastly regarding his companion while he did so. These preliminaries disposed of, he applied himself to teaching her the game, which she soon learnt tolerably well, being both sharp-witted and cunning.

"Now," said Mr. Swiveller, putting two sixpences into a saucer, and trimming the wretched candle, when the cards had been cut and dealt, "those are the stakes. If you win, you get 'em all. If I win, I get 'em. To make it seem more real and pleasant I shall call you the Marchioness, do you hear?"

The small servant nodded.

"Then, Marchioness," said Mr. Swiveller, "fire away!"

The Marchioness, holding her cards very tight in both hands, considered which to play, and Mr. Swiveller, assuming the gay and fashionable air which such society required, took another pull at the tankard, and waited for her to lead.

Mr. Swiveller and his partner played several rubbers, with varying success, until the loss of three sixpences, the gradual sinking of the purl and the striking of ten o'clock combined to render that gentleman mindful of the flight of time, and the expediency of withdrawing before Mr. Sampson and Miss Sally Brass returned.

"With which object in view, Marchioness," said Mr. Swiveller gravely, "I shall ask your ladyship's permission to put the board in my pocket, and to retire from the presence when I have finished this tankard ; merely observing, Marchioness, that since life like a river is flowing, I care not how fast it rolls on, ma'am, on, while such purl on the bank still is growing, and such eyes light the waves as they run. Marchioness, your health ! You will excuse my wearing my hat, but the palace is damp, and the marble floor is—if I may be allowed the expression—sloppy."

As a precaution against this latter inconvenience, Mr. Swiveller had been sitting for some time with his feet on the hob, in which attitude he now gave utterance to these apologetic observations, and slowly sipped the last choice drops of nectar.

"The Baron Sampsono Brasso and his fair sister are (you tell me) at the Play?" said Mr. Swiveller, leaning his left arm heavily upon the table, and raising his voice and his right leg after the manner of a theatrical bandit.

The Marchioness nodded.

"Ha !" said Mr. Swiveller with a portentous frown. "'Tis well, Marchioness !—but no matter. Some wine there.

"MARCHIONESS," SAID MR. SWIVELLER THOUGHTFULLY
"BE PLEASED TO DRAW NEARER"

Old Curiosity Shop

Ho!" He illustrated these melodramatic morsels by handing the tankard to himself with great humility, receiving it
haughtily, drinking from it thirstily, and smacking his lips
fiercely.

The small servant, who was not so well acquainted
with theatrical conventionalities as Mr. Swiveller (having,
indeed never seen a play or heard one spoken of, except by
some chance through chinks of doors and in other forbidden
places), was rather alarmed by demonstrations so novel in
their nature, and showed her concern so plainly in her looks
that Mr. Swiveller felt it necessary to discharge his brigand
manner for one more suitable to private life, as he asked:

"Do they often go where glory waits 'em, and leave you
here?"

"Oh, yes; I believe they do," returned the small servant.
"Miss Sallie's such a one-er for that, she is."

"Such a what?" said Dick.

"Such a one-er," returned the Marchioness.

After a moment's reflection, Mr. Swiveller determined
to forego his responsible duty of setting her right and to
suffer her to talk on, as it was evident that her tongue was
loosened by the purl and her opportunities for conversation
were not so frequent as to render a momentary check of little
consequence.

"They sometimes go to see Mr. Quilp," said the
small servant with a shrewd look; "they go to many places,
bless you."

"Is Mr. Brass a wunner?" said Dick.

"Not half what Miss Sally is, he isn't," replied the
small servant, shaking her head. "Bless you, he'd never do
anything without her."

"Oh! He wouldn't, wouldn't he?" said Dick.

"Miss Sally keeps him in such order," said the small servant, "he always asks her advice, he does; and he catches it sometimes. Bless you, you wouldn't believe how much he catches it."

"I suppose," said Dick, "that they consult together a good deal, and talk about a great many people—about me, for instance, sometimes, eh, Marchioness?"

The Marchioness nodded amazingly.

"Complimentary?" said Mr. Swiveller.

The Marchioness changed the motion of her head, which had not yet left off nodding, and suddenly began to shake it from side to side with a vehemence which threatened to dislocate her neck.

"Humph!" Dick muttered. "Would it be any breach of confidence, Marchioness, to relate what they say of the humble individual who has now the honor to——?"

"Miss Sallie says you're a funny chap," replied his friend.

"Well, Marchioness," said Swiveller, "that's not uncomplimentary. Merriment, Marchioness, is not a bad or degrading quality. Old King Cole was himself a merry old soul, if we may put any faith in the pages of history."

"But she says," pursued his companion, "that you ain't to be trusted."

"Why, really, Marchioness," said Mr. Swiveller thoughtfully; "several ladies and gentlemen—not exactly professional persons, but tradespeople, ma'am, tradespeople—have made the same remark. The obscure citizen who keeps the hotel over the way inclined strongly to that opinion tonight when I ordered him to prepare the banquet. It's a popular prejudice, Marchioness, and yet I am sure I don't know why, for I have been trusted in my time to a consider-

able amount, and I can safely say that I never forsook my
trust until it deserted me—never.   Mr. Brass is of the same
opinion, I suppose?"

His friend nodded again, with a cunning look which
seemed to hint that Mr. Brass held stronger opinions on the
subject than his sister; and seeming to recollect herself, added imploringly, "But don't you ever tell upon me, or I shall
be beat to death."

"Marchioness," said Mr. Swiveller, rising, "the word of
a gentleman is as good as his bond—sometimes better; as
in the present case, where his bond might prove but a doubtful sort of security.   I am your friend, and I hope we shall
play many more rubbers together in the same saloon.   But,
Marchioness," added Richard, stopping on his way to the
door, and wheeling slowly around upon the small servant,
who was following with the candle, "it occurs to me that
you must be in the constant habit of airing your eye at keyholes, to know all this."

"I only wanted," replied the trembling Marchioness,
"to know where the key of the safe was hid; that was all;
and I wouldn't have taken much, if I had found it—only
enough to squench my hunger."

"You didn't find it, then?" said Dick.   "But of course
you didn't, or you'd be plumper.   Good-night, Marchioness.
Fare thee well, and if forever, then forever fare thee well—
and put up the chain, Marchioness, in case of accidents."

With this parting injunction, Mr. Swiveller emerged
from the house, and feeling that he had by this time taken
quite as much to drink as promised to be good for his con-
stitution (purl being a rather strong and heady compound),
wisely resolved to betake himself to his lodgings, and to
bed at once.   Homeward he went therefore; and his apart

ments (for he still retained the plural fiction) being at no great distance from the office, he was soon seated in his own bed-chamber, where, having pulled off one boot and forgotten the other, he fell into deep cogitation.

"This Marchioness," said Mr. Swiveller, folding his arms, "is a very extraordinary person—surrounded by mys-teries, ignorant of the taste of beer, unacquainted with her own name (which is less remarkable), and taking a limited view of society through the keyholes of doors—can these things be her destiny, or has some unknown person started an opposition to the decrees of fate? It is a most inscrut-able and unmitigated staggerer!"

When his meditations had attained this satisfactory point, he became aware of his remaining boot, of which, with unimpaired solemnity, he proceeded to divest himself; shaking his head with exceeding gravity all the time, and sighing deeply.

"These rubbers," said Mr. Swiveller, putting on his nightcap in exactly the same style as he wore his hat, "re-mind me of the matrimonial fireside. My old girl, Chegg's wife, plays cribbage; all-fours alike. She rings the changes on 'em now. From sport to sport they hurry her, to banish her regrets, and when they win a smile from her they think that she forgets—but she don't. By this time, I should say," added Richard, getting his left cheek into profile, and looking complacently at the reflection of a very little scrap of whisker in the looking-glass; "by this time, I should say, the iron has entered into her soul. It serves her right."

Melting from this stern and obdurate into the tender and pathetic mood, Mr. Swiveller groaned a little, walked wildly up and down, and even made a show of tearing his hair, which however he thought better of, and wrenched the tassel from his nightcap instead. At last, undressing him-self with a gloomy resolution, he got into bed.

Some men, in his blighted position, would have taken to drinking; but as Mr Swiveller had taken to that before, he only took, on receiving the news that his girl was lost to him forever, to playing the flute; thinking, after mature con-sideration, that it was a good, sound, dismal occupation, not only in unison with his own sad thoughts, but calcu-lated to awaken a fellow-feeling in the bosom of his neigh-bors. In pursuance of this resolution, he now drew a little table to his bedside, and, arranging the light and a small oblong music-book to the best advantage, took his flute from its box and began to play most mournfully.

The air was "Away with melancholy"—a composition, which, when it is played very slowly on the flute in bed, with the further disadvantage of being performed by a gen-tleman but imperfectly acquainted with the instrument, who repeats one note a great many times before he can find the next, has not a lively effect. Yet for half the night, or more, Mr. Swiveller, lying sometimes on his back with his eyes upon the ceiling, and sometimes half out of bed to cor-rect himself by the book, played this unhappy tune over and over again; never leaving off, save for a minute or two at a time to take breath and soliloquize about the Marchioness, and then beginning again with renewed vigor. It was not until he had quite exhausted his several subjects of medita-tion, and had breathed into the flute the whole sentiment of the purl down to its very dregs, and had nearly maddened the people of the house, and at both the next doors, and over the way—that he shut up the music book, extinguished the candle, and, finding himself greatly lightened and re-lieved in his mind, turned round and fell asleep.

16

Dick continued his friendly relations towards the Marchioness, and when he fell ill with typhoid fever his little friend nursed him back to health. Just after this illness an aunt of his died and left him quite a large sum of money, a portion of which he used to educate the Marchioness, whom he afterwards married.